"Do You Know How Long It Would Take to Repay Ten Thousand Dollars?"

"I'll work for half pay," she cried, sensing a weakening. "I'll do anything you say."

He leaned back in his chair, arms crossed over his chest, regarding her insolently. "Anything?" he asked in a silken voice.

Her cheeks flamed as Jason's eyes wandered over her slender body, sending a chill of apprehension up her spine. But she nodded her head and said in a low voice, "Yes . . . anything."

"Well, now, that's very interesting. It just might provide a whole new solution. You said that I have everything I want, but that's not true. Suppose I were to tell you I want you?"

TRACY SINCLAIR
has worked extensively as a photojournalist. She's traveled throughout North America, as well as parts of the Caribbean, South America and Europe.

Dear Reader:

Silhouette Books is pleased to announce the creation of a new line of contemporary romances—*Silhouette Special Editions*. Each month we'll bring you six new love stories written by the best of today's authors— Janet Dailey, Brooke Hastings, Laura Hardy, Sondra Stanford, Linda Shaw, Patti Beckman, and many others.

Silhouette Special Editions are written with American women in mind; they are for readers who want more: more story, more details and descriptions, more realism, and more *romance*. *Special Editions* are longer than most contemporary romances allowing for a closer look at the relationship between hero and heroine with emphasis on heightened romantic tension and greater sensuous and sensual detail. If you want more from a romance, be sure to look for *Silhouette Special Editions* on sale this February wherever you buy books.

We welcome any suggestions or comments, and I invite you to write us at the address below.

Karen Solem
Editor-in-Chief
Silhouette Books
P.O. Box 769
New York, N. Y. 10019

TRACY SINCLAIR
Holiday in Jamaica

Silhouette Romance

Published by Silhouette Books New York

America's Publisher of Contemporary Romance

Other Silhouette Romances by Tracy Sinclair

Paradise Island

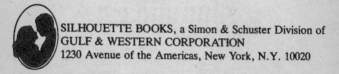

SILHOUETTE BOOKS, a Simon & Schuster Division of
GULF & WESTERN CORPORATION
1230 Avenue of the Americas, New York, N.Y. 10020

Copyright © 1981 by Tracy Sinclair

Distributed by Pocket Books

ISBN: 0-671-57123-0

First Silhouette Books printing December, 1981

10 9 8 7 6 5 4 3 2 1

America's Publisher of Contemporary Romance

Printed in the U.S.A.

Chapter One

A special hum of excitement ran through the big office, and Erin Brady looked up to see what was causing it. There were dozens of desks in the large room and an equal number of women occupying them, so a certain amount of chatter was always going on; but this was different. An underlying current of excitement had been added to the prosaic sounds of telephone and typewriter.

When she spied the big boss, Jason Dimitriou, stalking arrogantly through the room, the mystery was solved. Erin's soft mouth turned down disapprovingly. She could never understand the slavish adoration heaped on this man by every woman from eighteen to eighty.

Of course he was handsome; even she had to admit that. To start with, that tall, slim-hipped athlete's body made him stand out in any crowd. And those strange gray eyes, too thickly fringed with lashes for a mere male, were startling in his hawklike face. Add crisp black hair that fell carelessly across a tanned forehead and you had the sex appeal of a Hollywood actor. But that was the whole point. It would make just as much sense to fall in love with a movie star. How could every woman in the office be crazy about a man who barely knew she was alive?

Look at him now, for instance, striding imperiously by like a Greek god, oblivious to all the attention he was generating. Or maybe he was just used to it, since it happened wherever he went.

At thirty-two, Jason Dimitriou was already a legend, the darling of society columnists and gossip writers alike, who documented his every activity. It was common knowledge that he had taken over his grandfather's shipping line while still in his twenties and had built it into an empire encompassing everything from tankers to cruise ships and a multitude of allied enterprises as well. Now it was his personal life that the media was interested in, and they dogged his footsteps, each reporter hoping for a scoop when the playboy bachelor took a wife. So far, they had all been disappointed.

He appeared at every glittering function, and photographers couldn't seem to get enough pictures of him. But the dazzling women clinging tightly to his arm changed as rapidly as the seasons.

Erin's brother Bob was only a junior accountant at Dimitriou Shipping Lines, but he longed to emulate this flamboyant life-style. Avidly observing every movement of his illustrious boss, he tried to pattern himself along the same lines.

Bob Brady was only twenty-five, but he already considered himself the complete sophisticate. Only the absence of sufficient funds separated him from the good things in life to which he felt entitled. His job at DSL wasn't as challenging as he would have liked and didn't pay nearly enough to provide all the luxuries he craved. But it was a good job with a promising future, as his sister kept reminding him, although she wasn't interested in the business world herself. In fact, if anyone had told Erin that the day would soon come when she would join Bob as a Dimitriou employee, they would both have laughed.

Erin's future had been headed in an entirely different direction. She was in her first year at college and, with the confidence of youth, had her whole life mapped out. She was an art history major and would go on to graduate school after her degree and from there to a good job in a museum. Her entire future stretched happily ahead like a broad highway with no detours.

Even Bob's disapproval didn't shake her determination. She had always adored her older brother and accepted his word as law, especially after their father died. But this was the one thing on which they disagreed.

"Why would you want to work in some dusty old museum?" he asked. "There's no money in it, that's for sure."

"There is more to life than money," she protested.

"Name three things," he scoffed. "And besides that, who are you ever going to meet? The kinds of guys who work in places like that wear sweaters with suede patches on the elbows." With an unconscious reflex, he smoothed down the lapels of his new Italian jacket.

"I'm not looking for a husband," Erin said indignantly. "If I meet somebody, fine; but I'm going to prepare myself for a career in the meantime."

"Mother, can't you talk some sense into her head?" Bob asked disgustedly. "First thing you know, we're going to wind up with an old maid on our hands."

Mrs. Brady smilingly shook her head, refusing to get drawn into this running argument. It was her private opinion, which she was careful not to voice, that Erin would be married long before she finished college, in spite of her statements to the contrary.

Gazing at her daughter, she marveled at this delicate beauty as she did every time she took a good look at her. The Brady clan was presentable enough but had never before produced a child of such breathtaking loveliness. She studied the long auburn hair, the color of maple leaves in late autumn, and the deep blue eyes, slightly tilted at the corners, giving their owner a wide-eyed, breathless look. The creamy skin was flushed a soft pink now from the earnestness of her argument, and Mrs. Brady smiled. No, they didn't have to worry about this girl. Her future was assured.

But Fate dislikes being taken for granted, and, almost overnight, Erin's world fell apart. It began when her mother became sick and died after a very short illness. While she and Bob were still in a state of shock, the attorney called them into his office and talked a great deal of mumbo jumbo. There were papers to sign and explanations, none of which made much sense. The upshot was that there was no money left.

About the only thing remaining was the modest family home, but it was heavily mortgaged. The lawyer advised them that they would be better off living there and meeting the payments rather than trying to sell it and having to pay rent somewhere else. It went without saying that Erin would have to drop out of college and get a job. The problem was, where? With no experience and no prospects, the future looked decidedly grim until Bob got her a job in the steno pool at DSL.

At first she was so numb with grief over her mother and the collapse of her own dreams that nothing else seemed to matter. She was like a sleepwalker groping her way through an endless night. It was a dark period, but gradually Erin's naturally sunny nature surfaced and she began to take an interest in life once more. Everyone was delighted to see her smile again, and the women at the office went out of their way to be helpful. They took a personal interest in teaching her the routine and warning her of possible pitfalls.

"The one to watch out for is Harry Martin. He's our resident wolf," Melissa Jones cautioned almost immediately.

Before Erin could ask the obvious question, Terry Turnbull said, "He's the office manager. If he ever calls you in, be sure to keep the door open."

Erin laughed. "You must be exaggerating. Surely he wouldn't try anything at work."

"Well, maybe not," Mary Gordon admitted grudgingly, "but if he ever asks you for a date—don't go!"

Erin had seen Harry Martin, a flashy dresser with an overly friendly manner and something rather suggestive in his eye. It was obvious that he considered himself a lady-killer. Maybe he appealed to some girls, but he certainly wasn't her type. Nor was Jason Dimitriou.

"Do you mean to say you don't think he's the most handsome man you've ever seen in real life?" Terry demanded.

"Oh, he's handsome enough," Erin admitted reluctantly, "but he knows it. I don't like conceited men."

"What makes you think he's conceited? You've never even talked to him."

"But that's just it. He walks through this office with his nose in the air, as if we didn't even exist."

"Erin, he's involved in business deals all over the world," Terry said impatiently. "He's probably juggling millions of dollars in his head. Can you blame him for being preoccupied?"

Erin stuck out her lower lip stubbornly. "Well, he

could say good morning or at least smile or something. I'll bet he's a real tyrant to work for."

"Not according to Helen," Melissa disagreed. "You should hear her sing his praises, and I don't think it's just out of loyalty to the boss."

Helen Demarest was Jason's private secretary, and Mary looked thoughtful. "I wonder if there's anything going on between those two?"

"That's a terrible thing to say," Erin protested. "Helen is a wonderful secretary and a lovely person. I don't think you should start any rumors."

"Since you've only been here three months, how did you get to be such an authority on Helen?" Terry asked with some asperity. "I didn't know you knew her that well."

"I don't, really. I've spoken to her a couple of times, but she seems very nice," Erin defended herself. "Just the other day I made a mistake on a report she gave me to type for Mr. Dimitriou, and, instead of bawling me out, she stalled him until I had a chance to do it over. I bet he'd have a fit if he knew."

Their opinion of Jason was the only thing they really differed on, and Erin was grateful to the women for all their help. It was a pleasant office and the working conditions were good. She realized things could have been a lot worse.

Another convenient thing about working for DSL was the fact that she and Bob could drive to and from work together. It was a nice way to start the day, as she didn't get to see much of him otherwise. Bob spent very little of his free time at home.

One morning a few days before Christmas, they were on their way to the office as usual. The sun shone down from a cloudless blue sky and it didn't seem like December. Miami was filled with tourists methodically basting their bodies so they would have a suntan to show to their less fortunate friends shivering in the northern snows, and the weather was cooperating enthusiastically.

As they crossed the causeway, Erin looked at the sleek luxury crafts bobbing at anchor in the bay. "Isn't it a gorgeous day?" she remarked.

Bob spared a quick look at the regal homes on Shell Island, their velvety green lawns rolling down to the water's edge. Scowling, he said, "A fat lot of good it does *us*. We might as well be a couple of slaves going off to the salt mines."

Erin looked at her brother curiously. "I thought you liked your job. Is something the matter or did you just get up on the wrong side of the bed this morning?"

"Oh, the job's okay, I guess, but I'm tired of working at a desk. I want to be out there where the action is." He took one hand off the wheel and gestured expansively at the trim yachts. "If I weren't stuck in an office all day, I could be out there water-skiing, or on a plane to Paris or—oh, you know. What's the point in waiting until you're too old to enjoy things? If I just had more money . . ." His voice trailed off.

"You're still awfully young," Erin said to console him, but he took immediate offense.

"Oh, no, not you, too! Every time I ask for more responsibility at the office, I get that same line. 'You're young, Bob, have a little patience, your day will come.'" His voice was a bitter mimicry. "Why am I the one who has to wait while guys like Jason Dimitriou are born with silver spoons in their mouths? Have you seen pictures of that mansion he lives in or the car he drives?"

Erin's soft mouth thinned in disapproval. "As far

as I'm concerned, that silver spoon tarnished his whole personality. If that's what money does for you, then I'm glad you don't have any."

"What do you mean?"

"I think he's a creep, that's what I mean."

Bob looked at her incredulously. "Do you mean to say you're not bananas over him like every other female in that office?"

"I think he's arrogant and rude, and it's just fine with me that he doesn't know we lowly women in the steno pool are even alive. Does that answer your question?" she asked scornfully.

"Yes, but you're wrong about one thing, I can tell you. He's aware of everything that goes on in that office, even if he isn't exactly the glad-handing type. As a matter of fact, he's really a nice guy when you get to know him, although I'll admit he's kind of formidable. They let me sit in as a trainee on a few conferences he held, and he's an all-right Joe as long as you don't try to con him. One of the men tried to bluff about some reports he hadn't done, and I thought the roof was going to fall on the guy. But if you're straight with him, he's something else."

"Well, you're certainly changing your tune, aren't you? A minute ago you were complaining he was just a rich playboy."

"That's not exactly what I said, although he sure is that," Bob commented appreciatively.

"How can you admire a man with a reputation like he has?" Erin cried.

He grinned at her. "It isn't admiration so much as envy."

"Oh, you men, you're all alike!" They had reached the office, and Erin flounced angrily out of the car. "I'll see you tonight," she called over her shoulder.

The day's work was already piled on her desk, and the top sheet had a red flag pasted to it, denoting a rush job. Speak of the devil, Erin thought. The note clipped to the page was from Helen Demarest informing her that the report was for the big boss himself and was to be delivered as soon as it was ready. She rolled a piece of paper into the typewriter and set to work.

When the job was done, Erin stapled the pages together, pushed her chair back and started for the executive offices.

Terry hailed her. "Where are you going, woman? It's too early for a coffee break."

"I have to deliver a report to The Great One."

"How did you get so lucky? Can I go in your place?"

Erin grinned and continued on without answering. If she were truly lucky, he wouldn't be in yet, she reflected. Not that it mattered one way or another. She would just give the papers to his secretary and be in and out in nothing flat. But when she entered the executive suite, Helen Demarest wasn't there.

Erin hesitated. Should she put the papers on her desk and leave? But the note had indicated it was urgent, and she hadn't even seen Helen this morning. Suppose she was out sick or at the dentist or something? Erin preferred not to dwell on what would happen if he didn't get his report and she was the one responsible.

Taking a deep breath, she started down the corridor to Jason Dimitriou's big office, checking over the pages one last time as she went. There were voices coming from his office, but they didn't penetrate her consciousness until she reached the door and realized something was wrong—terribly wrong!

Helen was crumpled in a chair by the desk, her

head cushioned on her arms, sobbing as though her heart would break. Jason stood at the window with his back to the room.

"It's up to you," he was saying, in a voice tight with repressed emotion. "You can either keep the baby or put it up for adoption. Don't worry, I'll take care of everything. But for your own sake, I'd strongly urge that you give it up."

Helen responded in a strangled voice that was almost incoherent. He evidently understood her, for he answered, "You mustn't let this ruin your life; these things happen." Turning abruptly, he spotted Erin standing uncertainly in the doorway. For a moment they just stared at each other, and then, scowling ferociously, he asked, "What are you doing here?"

She was rooted to the spot and could barely find her voice. "I—I just came to deliver this report."

He crossed the room in a few giant steps and towered over her threateningly. She could almost feel the repressed fury in his powerful body. "How long have you been standing there?" he demanded.

"I just got here," Erin lied, praying he would believe her.

He scanned her face suspiciously. "How much did you hear?"

"Noth—nothing," she said, starting to back away, but a long arm shot out and his steely fingers bit into her shoulder, drawing her so close their bodies almost touched. Realizing she couldn't completely ignore the tableau right in front of her eyes, she added, "I heard Miss Demarest crying, but I . . . didn't want to intrude. I hope nothing's wrong."

He continued to stare at her, and his stormy gray eyes seemed to be looking into her very soul. Finally she whispered, "You're hurting me."

He loosened his hold abruptly, as though unaware until then of what he was doing, and Erin added in a little rush, "Is she ill? Is there anything I can do?"

He turned away from her and looked somberly at Helen. "No, she's just had some . . . rather upsetting news. Her grandmother in California is ill, and Helen is going to take a leave of absence."

"I'm so sorry," Erin managed.

"Yes, well, you can go back to your desk now." He looked at her impassively, obviously speculating on just how much she had heard and daring her to make use of it.

Erin accepted her release gratefully and fled down the corridor, trying to outrace her thoughts. Unable to face anyone yet, she ducked into the ladies room to hide until she could compose herself. Her mind was spinning, filled with anger and fear and an aching compassion. The sight of Helen—that bright, charming, friendly woman—sobbing in despair was burned into her brain. How could women be such fools over men? Jason Dimitriou's callous words still assaulted her ears. "Don't worry, I'll take care of everything," and "these things happen." The man was a monster! Did he think his money could buy him out of every moral responsibility? The worst of it was, it could. He ought to be arrested, but unfortunately it wasn't a crime to take advantage of a gullible girl.

Just yesterday they were discussing Helen's devotion to him. Remembering Mary's speculation about a possible relationship and how indignantly she had defended the other girl, Erin realized sadly how much she had to learn about life. But Helen was older and should have been wiser. How had she allowed this to happen? Didn't she know that a man with a reputation like his was only interested in a brief tawdry little affair? What was his power over women that they were willing to submit to him against all reason?

Maybe a few brief moments in his arms made it all worthwhile. Unbidden, his image appeared before her—that splendid body radiating masculinity. She was ashamed to admit it, but just being close to him had quickened her senses; the rapid beat of her heart was caused by more than fear.

She closed her eyes, seeking to drive away his hateful presence. Was it any wonder he was so successful when even Erin, who despised him, could be disturbed by his mere proximity? The sound of the door opening caused her to jump guiltily.

It was Terry Turnbull who glanced at her in surprise. "What are you doing here? I thought you had such a rush errand."

Erin looked at the papers still clutched in her hand and realized she would have to go back and leave them on Helen's desk. Her heart sank, but she tried to keep her voice natural as she answered, "That's where I'm headed now."

"You left ten minutes ago. What have you been doing?" Terry scrutinized her curiously. "One of the women heard there was something funny going on around here. Do you know what it's all about?"

It didn't take long for gossip to start, did it? Poor Helen—the news would be all over the office like a flash flood. It wasn't that they were cruel or unfeeling, but when a bunch of women are gathered together every day from nine until five, they're bound to take a proprietary interest in every little thing that happens. And this was far from a little thing. Would he think Erin had spread the news? It was a dreadful possibility. She would have to be terribly careful!

Turning toward the door, she said lightly, "I

haven't the slightest idea what you're talking about, and I'd better deliver this report pronto."

Erin was quiet in the car going home that night, but her brother didn't seem to notice. His bad mood of the morning had completely vanished, to be replaced by a kind of repressed excitement. He kept giving her sidelong looks, waiting for her to ask the usual questions about his day. Although he rambled on about trivial things, Erin would have seen, if she hadn't been so preoccupied, that he was clearly bursting with news. When she merely answered in monosyllables, he finally asked, "What's wrong? You look sunk. Did something happen at work today?"

"No, I'm fine; you're the surprising one. Wasn't it just this morning you were singing mood indigo? What happened to brighten your day?"

He laughed. "Oh, you know me. I never stay down for long. Something always seems to turn up when you least expect it."

"What was it this time?" Even when she was upset, Erin could always manage to be interested in anything that concerned her brother.

"It was the darndest thing. You know how sometimes you feel like you're at a dead end and all of a sudden somebody puts a road map in your hand? Well, this morning, Mr. Dimitriou called me into his office and—"

Erin sat up very straight in her seat. "If it concerns that man, I don't want to hear it."

"'That man,' as you call him, happens to be our boss, remember?" he asked dryly.

"Not mine for very long, I hope. I'm going to start looking for another job."

Bob was so startled he inadvertently slammed on the brakes, almost causing an accident. Over the blare of angry horns he asked, "Are you crazy?"

"I don't think so," she answered grimly. "I just want out."

"Why all of a sudden?"

"Never mind, I just do," she told him.

"Where do you think you'll get another job?"

"I'll find something," she promised.

"Are you kidding? You were lucky to get this one with no experience. They only took you on because I happened to know the personnel manager and he was sorry for us. If you quit after just three months, who do you think is going to hire you? Or do you expect him to give you a reference?" he asked sarcastically.

The worst of it was, he was right and she knew it. At least for the time being, she was trapped at DSL because she couldn't afford the luxury of unemployment. But it was going to be torture!

"I'm not trying to be mean, Erin," Bob said earnestly. "I'm just pointing out the hard facts."

Making a face, she said grudgingly, "Oh, all right."

He was not fully convinced. "Promise me you won't do anything foolish," he urged.

"I said all right," she muttered rebelliously. "Let's change the subject. Can you be ready by six o'clock? I'd like to get to Aunt Ellen's a little early."

"Tonight?" He gave her a startled look. "I can't go anywhere with you tonight. I have a date."

"Robert Brady, are you trying to be exasperating or just doing it accidentally?"

After the kind of day she had had, this was the final straw. Although the last thing in the world she felt like doing was going to a party, they had accepted this date weeks ago. But even if the invitation had arrived this morning, it would have carried the same obligation. Aunt Ellen was the closest thing they had to a relative, and, besides being their godmother, she was their favorite person.

When they were small, Aunt Ellen could always be counted on for ice cream bars and Saturday movie money. When they got older, she was a successful mediator of parental prohibitions like using the family car for a date or wearing high heels to school. Erin enumerated all these things plus more, ending with the fact that Aunt Ellen was expecting them, and Bob had better know that his little sister wasn't going to make excuses for him anymore.

He was somewhat taken aback by her vehemence. "You don't have to get so steamed about it. I just forgot, that's all, and I have this date. . . ."

"Well, I guess you could bring her. I'm sure Aunt Ellen wouldn't mind."

"It isn't that kind of date. I've been invited to a party." His eyes narrowed in thought and he stole a sideways look at her. Evidently making up his mind about something, he said, "Forget it. I'll be ready."

Erin selected a plum-colored dirndl skirt and a cream-colored silk blouse with long full sleeves and a wide, ruffled, drawstring neck that tied over one shoulder in a tiny self bow. Picking up a matching jacket and a small satin purse, she headed for the door, satisfied that she looked presentable. The outfit wasn't new—there wasn't money for that sort of thing now—but it was well made and looked kind of Christmasy.

Bob was waiting for her, and, instead of being sullen about having to give up his plans as Erin had feared, he was remarkably cheerful. She felt a pang of guilt. His well-being was always paramount in her mind, just as his approval was absolutely essential. She vowed to make it up to him and tried to be especially entertaining on the short drive to their godmother's. Whether she diverted him or not was questionable, but Erin gave him such full attention that she didn't notice they were driving through unfamiliar streets. It was only when he crossed the short bridge onto one of the lush islands off the causeway that she realized they had taken the wrong route.

"Where are we, Bob? This isn't the way to Aunt Ellen's."

He pulled up in front of a sprawling white mansion and cut the motor. "I have to make a stop first."

"What do you mean? Where are we?"

He turned to face her. In the muted light from a street lamp, his jaw was set. "Look, Erin, I said I'd go with you to Aunt Ellen's and I will. But first you have to stop off at a party with me. That's fair, isn't it?"

"I don't even know where we are," she said, bewildered by this turn of events.

His eyes didn't quite meet hers as he said, "I was going to tell you on the way home from work today, but you were so worked up about Mr. Dimitriou that I figured this way would be better."

"Do you mean—"

"Yes, this is his house. He's the one who invited me to the party." When she would have interrupted, he dismissed her protests. "Listen, Erin, this means a lot to me. Mr. Dimitriou called me into his office today and said he was having a little Christmas gathering for a select group in the company."

"He said that?" she asked incredulously.

"Well, he didn't exactly put it that way, but that was the general idea. He even told me to call him Jason. That's going to take a little getting used to," Bob mused in an awed tone of voice. "He said he wanted to get to know his people better. So you can see now why I had to come, can't you? It's almost a command performance."

"It seems to me he knows some of his people too well already," Erin snapped.

"What's that supposed to mean?"

"Oh, never mind," she told him, and muttered almost to herself, "His conscience is probably bothering him. He's decided to be nice to the little people."

"Listen, I don't know what's eating you, but we're going inside and that's final!"

"Nothing in this world could induce me to step foot in that house," Erin cried. But when confronted by his very real anger, she added in a softer tone, "Besides, he didn't invite *me*, so it wouldn't even be right."

"He told me I could bring a date if I wanted," he assured her. "What's the difference if I bring my sister instead?"

They discussed it heatedly, but Erin could tell this was an argument she had no chance of winning. And in spite of her anger over his deception, she could understand her brother's jubilation at the invitation. Maybe it really was the long-awaited break. Maybe they had their eye on him and he was being considered for a better position. She mustn't let her prejudice jeopardize his chances.

"Bob, I hope this means as much as you think it does. You know I wish you all the luck in the world—and you're going to need it working for that man." She couldn't help adding, "But I . . . just think it would be better if you went without me. I'll wait here in the car for you."

"Are you out of your mind? There will be people going in and out, high-level people that I should get to know. What are they going to think when they see you sitting here in the car? They're bound to think it was my idea because no sensible person would *choose* to wait outside when there's a party going on inside."

"How would they know I'm waiting for you?"

"Are you kidding? Who else in that crowd drives a five-year-old sedan?"

"Nobody has to see me. I'll scrunch down in the corner," Erin told him, not very hopefully in the face of his disgusted look.

They argued the point at length. When he finally threatened not to take her to Aunt Ellen's at all, she knew she was beaten. There was no other transportation within miles, and Bob was capable of carrying out his threat.

Erin followed her brother up the long path to the stately front doors, dragging her feet as much as she dared. A butler answered his ring, and they found themselves in a massive entrance hall with a gleaming floor of polished marble. A graceful curving staircase was opposite the entry, and sounds of revelry were coming from a room on the left. After taking her wrap, the butler ushered them into the largest living room Erin had ever seen. There were so many people present that it was difficult to fully appreciate the exquisite furnishings. She got the impression of heavy sea-foam drapes and luxurious damask sofas and chairs scattered throughout the room. In the far corner was a huge grand piano that was perfectly in keeping with the scale of this massive salon.

A few people were gathered around a man who was seated at the piano playing soft music, but most of the others were chatting in small or large groups. A white-coated waiter carrying a tray of champagne cocktails paused to offer them one. Their host—or, rather, Bob's host, Erin corrected herself—was nowhere in sight.

"I don't know a soul here, do you?" she whispered.

"Well, I know a few people by sight but nobody to actually go up and say hello to."

At his tone, she glanced up and saw that he looked as lost and lonely as she felt. For all his bravado and pretended sophistication, Erin could tell he was out of his element in this glittering gathering. She wanted to slip her hand in his for comfort. We're like two little waifs with our noses pressed against the candy-store window, she thought wryly. Maybe now he'll realize we don't belong here. If I can just convince him to have this drink and go, we won't get to Aunt Ellen's too late after all.

But before she could frame her suggestion in a tactful way, they were hailed by a man who obviously belonged at this party. His suit was a mastery of understated elegance—in fact, everything about his attire was impeccable—but it was his casually assured manner that stamped him a member of Jason Dimitriou's crowd.

"Hello, I don't believe I've seen you around here before. In fact, I'm certain of it. Please tell me you're not a tourist who's going to disappear in the morning. I couldn't bear the disappointment." His hazel eyes laughed down at Erin out of a bronzed face crowned by sun-bleached hair. Almost as an afterthought, the gaze flickered over to Bob—but only for a moment. "I'm Bradford Honeywell," he added.

Before Erin could respond, her brother answered for both of them. "It's nice to know you. I'm Robert Brady and this is my sister, Erin."

Honeywell's face lit up and his manner became

expansive, openly including Bob this time. "Oh! Brother and sister, isn't that nice. Are you both friends of Jason's?"

Erin thought she detected a special questioning note as he looked at her. He's probably trying to find out in a subtle way if I'm one of Mr. Dimitriou's women, she thought with distaste. Before she could frame a suitable reply, Bob answered for her.

"I'm associated in business with Jason," he said, "and Erin is my guest this evening."

That was marginally true, of course, but it made her uneasy. To give the impression that he held a big position at DSL seemed unwise. And why hadn't Bob mentioned that she worked there, too? Their jobs might not be very grand, but they were nothing to be ashamed of. However, Erin remained uncomfortably silent, as he knew she would.

"Well, that's just great," their new-found friend said heartily. "I wonder why I haven't met you before?" Bob was spared an answer as Brad turned to Erin, saying, "We have a lot of time to make up. Why don't we go over there in the corner and get acquainted?"

"The three of us?" she asked mischievously.

"They say three's a crowd," he drawled. "Besides, I'm sure brother Bob is dying to say hello to some of his friends."

She stole a look at her brother's face and saw panic there at the prospect of being left all alone in this alien environment. It would serve him right, Erin thought. But she couldn't do it to him, so she smiled sweetly and said, "Even though we're related, he's still my date. I don't think I should leave him."

"All right, if you say so, but at least let's get out of the doorway." Brad seemed to understand and

accept her answer with good grace. Putting a casual
arm around her shoulders, he propelled her gently
into the room. "You look like you have one foot out
the door, and I don't intend to let you get away that
easily."

"As a matter of fact, we can only stay a short
time," she told him, ignoring her brother's scowl.
"We're due at another party."

"You don't have to impress me with your popular-
ity; I can tell that by looking at you," Brad said, his
eyes wandering appreciatively over her.

Erin colored self-consciously. "I didn't mean it
to sound that way. It's just that we have this other
appointment."

"But we don't have to leave yet," Bob added
hastily.

"That's good, because there are some people you
really should meet," and he led them to a group of
men and women who were chatting together in the
middle of the room.

When the introductions were made, Erin recognized several of the men as business associates of
Jason Dimitriou's. One was a vice president at DSL
and another was the head of a bank. There was also
a beautiful woman whose name appeared often in
the society columns.

Erin wondered what these people would think if
they knew who the Bradys really were. It worried
her that they were here under slightly false pretenses, but the thought evidently didn't occur to Bob.
He expanded visibly in this rarefied atmosphere.

"Now that big brother is adequately launched,
why don't we go for a stroll in the moonlight?" Brad
whispered in her ear.

She turned smilingly toward him, but the feeling
of being watched made her glance over his shoulder,

straight into the eyes of Jason Dimitriou, who was standing across the room, his smoldering gaze riveted on her. Even from a distance, she could tell that he was furiously angry. Erin had felt he wouldn't be pleased to find her in his home, but she didn't expect such a violent reaction. A pulse started to throb in her temple. It was madness to come here. Why hadn't Bob listened to her? Now they would be unmasked in front of everyone! He looked angry enough to say anything.

As he cut through the crowd, tall and elegant in cream-colored flannels and a dark jacket with a silk ascot knotted carelessly around his tanned throat, Erin started to tremble and look around for some means of escape. It was impossible, of course, because she was hemmed in by the other guests. And then he was there, looming over her, his gray eyes narrowed and dangerous.

"What are you doing here?" he demanded curtly.

"Come on, Jason, is that any way to talk to a lady?" Brad asked.

"Stay out of this," Jason ordered. He had deliberately kept his voice low so that no one except Brad heard his abrupt words to Erin.

"Now just a minute—" Brad protested, but Jason grabbed her by the wrist and practically dragged her after him through a set of tall French doors onto a wide patio.

There was a magnificent garden beyond the terrace, illuminated by moonlight and low spotlights hidden in the shrubbery. Whitewashed brick paths wound around hibiscus bushes covered with pink and red blossoms, which contrasted colorfully with fragrant gardenias gleaming whitely against dark green leaves like dozens of corsages attached by an artful florist. It was a scene of surpassing beauty, but

Erin didn't have time to enjoy it because her host was in a towering rage.

"All right, let's have it. Why did you come here?" he repeated.

"You're hurting my wrist," she protested.

Instead of releasing her, he increased the pressure, and she winced with pain. His fingers tightened around her like a vise. "What are you trying to pull, a little spot of blackmail?"

"I don't know what you're talking about!" she cried.

"Don't you?" he sneered.

"No, I don't, and I'll thank you to take your hands off me!" Erin's temper was rising as the pain in her wrist increased. "Is this the way you treat all your guests?" When he looked at her blankly, she said, "Well, maybe I wasn't exactly invited, but Bob said it would be all right. I'm sorry if he was wrong, but you have no right to manhandle me like this."

"What are you talking about? Bob? Bob who?" Some of his anger ebbed and he was clearly puzzled.

"My brother, Robert Brady. He works for you in the accounting department, and he said you invited him here tonight."

"Good Lord! Are you Brady's sister?" At her nod, his fingers finally loosed their aching grip and he said, "It seems I owe you an apology—" He broke off and looked searchingly at her. "Wait a minute. You're the girl who was in my office this morning. I know I'm not wrong about *that*."

This was the moment she had been dreading. Unless she could convince him that she hadn't heard anything that went on between Helen and him, it wasn't only her job that was at stake; more importantly, Bob might lose his as well. She could tell just by looking at this man that he was a vengeful enemy.

Since her brother had brought her into the company, he would come in for a share of the blame. Erin was determined that mustn't happen.

Managing a rueful smile, she said, "I work for DSL, too, but only in the stenographic pool. You have so many employees that it's no wonder you didn't know I was one of them. But how nice of you to remember seeing me this morning."

"I remember all right," he said grimly. "If you're in the pool, what were you doing in my office?"

"Miss Demarest gave me a rush report to type for you, and when she wasn't at her desk, I thought I'd better bring it in." Giving him what she hoped was a guileless look, she went on, "It's too bad about her grandmother. I hope everything's going to be all right."

He inspected her face intently while she held her breath waiting for the verdict. After a moment that seemed like an eternity, he relaxed, reasonably convinced that she was as innocent as she looked.

"I'm sure she'll be fine," he answered finally.

"Oh, I'm so glad," Erin breathed. "Helen is a dear woman."

The last of his suspicion seemed to dissipate as he said, "I thought you . . . I mean . . . well, it seems I owe you an apology."

"Not at all, she said hastily. "Gate-crashers are an abomination, and I quite understand how you would feel if I gave you that impression."

"No, my behavior was inexcusable. You must let me make it up to you."

"It isn't necessary," she insisted. Her heart was racing after the close call, and she wanted to get away before anything happened to change his mind. Turning toward the house, she said, "I'm afraid I've kept you from your guests too long already."

But Jason's mood had undergone a lightning

change once his misgivings were satisfied. He was looking at her now the way a man looks at a beautiful woman.

"Don't go. I don't even know your first name," he said.

"It's Erin."

"That's a very lovely name."

"Thank you." Feeling extremely flustered under his smiling gaze, she looked yearningly at the brightly lit party just beyond the French doors. "I really must go."

He reached out to take her hand, and, almost instinctively, she flinched away from him. His eyes were grave as he reached for her again, cupping her shoulders in a gentle grasp. "You're afraid of me, aren't you?"

"No, I . . . it's just—"

"You mustn't be afraid, little Erin. I won't hurt you."

He bent his head toward her, and she was drowning in the magnetism of those strange gray eyes. Come to me my love, they seemed to say. It was a temptation to relax in the circle of those strong arms and feel them close around her. But as she swayed toward him, an image of Helen Demarest the way she looked the last time Erin had seen her flashed through her mind. Did it start like this for her, too?

With a tiny gasp, Erin stepped back from his embrace. "Your guests will never forgive me for monopolizing you this way," she said shakily.

He gave a tiny chuckle but made no move to possess her again. "They'll never miss me as long as the champagne holds out."

"That isn't a very nice way to talk about your friends," she chided, her breathing still rather uneven.

"You're right, of course, and I stand corrected.

But do I detect a note of criticism in your voice?" He raised one eyebrow. "It sounds like you don't approve of me very much."

Erin would have given a week's pay to tell him exactly what she did think of him. Managing to keep her tone neutral, she said, "I wouldn't presume to disapprove of the boss."

He frowned. "I'm not your boss tonight. I'm a man you've just met who wants to get to know you. Come, we'll walk in the garden." He took her hand and held onto it when she tried to pull away. "Tell me all about yourself."

Erin inhaled the perfumed air before shaking her head. "It wouldn't be a very interesting story."

"I can scarcely believe that." He broke off a huge pink cabbage rose and gently stroked her cheek with it before handing it to her. "Although I can see you haven't had time for much living yet. How old are you, anyway?"

"I'm nineteen."

"My goodness, that old?" he asked, his eyes dancing with merriment. "And what do you want to be when you grow up?"

He said it as though it were a big joke—as if she were some bubble-headed little thing without a thought for the future, and was only working at DSL as a lark. It probably never occurred to him that anyone would do something she didn't want to do, since all the people he knew did exactly as they pleased. But thinking of her hopeless ambitions and the dull routine of her unimportant job, Erin felt inexpressibly sad. What was she doing here with this man, anyway? Even if she wanted to explain, which she didn't, he would never understand. She raised her head, prepared to say something suitably flip. Instead, she found herself looking into eyes that were devoid now of mockery.

"What's the matter, little one?" he asked gently.

Unexpected tears threatened at his soft tone, and for just a moment she felt comforted by his sympathy. But then her common sense returned. This solicitous pose was all part of the same act. Looking into that ruggedly handsome face, even she, who knew better, could almost believe he was sincere. But Erin wasn't about to become just another notch on his belt.

Resolutely, she said, "Nothing's wrong. It's just that I really do have to leave."

"So early?"

"Yes, I'm sorry. I have to go to a party at my aunt's, and I'm terribly late already. I know Bob is going to be furious with me for dragging him away, but I really must go."

"Then let me drive you."

"Oh, no, I couldn't possibly!" Was there no way to get away from this man?

"It's the only sensible solution if you're sure you have to leave." At her nod, he continued, "There's no reason to spoil Bob's evening. Besides, I bought myself a new toy for Christmas, and I'd like to try it out."

"A new toy?"

"An Aston-Martin." In answer to her blank look, he said, "It's a make of car."

Her brother would have known immediately what Jason was talking about, but Erin could be excused her ignorance since it was unlikely she would be acquainted with a car costing that much money.

"That's nice," she answered politely, and Jason grinned, realizing she had no idea of its value. "But I still can't let you—"

"I don't want to hear any arguments, it's all settled," he cut in. "We don't even have to go back in the house. We can get to the garage this way."

Putting his arm around her shoulders, he urged her along the path.

"But my brother—I have to at least tell him I'm leaving." Too late, Erin realized she had given tacit agreement, but there didn't seem to be anything else she could do. His high-handed manner brooked no argument.

"Don't worry. I'll tell him when I get back. If I know brothers, he probably won't even know you've gone. There are a lot of attractive ladies in there."

He was right, of course. Bob was undoubtedly having the time of his life and would think she was crazy for not being delighted that his boss was giving her all this attention. But the gentle pressure of Jason's arm was provoking all kinds of conflicting emotions.

There was no doubt about the man's pure animal attraction, which made him all the more dangerous. Erin was uncomfortably aware of that hard, lean body so close to hers and of the firm arm holding her an unwilling prisoner. She breathed a soft sigh of relief when they finally reached the huge garage and he helped her into a long, sleek sports job, one of the many cars it held.

As the powerful motor purred into action and roared down the driveway, Jason gave it his full attention. He did indeed seem like a child with a new toy, but Erin didn't allow herself to be fooled. There was very little of the boy in this complex man.

Soon they were on the causeway with the lights of the city in front of them and neon-lit Miami Beach with its multimillion-dollar hotels in back. The water glittered blackly on either side of the broad road, and Erin watched in fascination as Jason's strong hands steered the sleek car skillfully in and out of traffic. There was a feeling of repressed excitement about him, as though he enjoyed his mastery over those scores of surging horses under the hood. Erin shivered without quite knowing why.

She could have sworn that his full attention was on the road, but he noticed her involuntary movement and immediately asked, "Are you cold?"

"No . . . no, I'm fine."

He turned his head for a moment and smiled at her. "You certainly are."

Erin flushed but managed to say quite casually, "And you're very charming."

In one of his swift changes of mood, he suddenly became serious. "I try to be, but I'm afraid I said something to upset you back there in the garden."

"It was nothing, really."

"Are you sure?"

She nodded her head.

"No dark secrets in your past?"

This time she laughed and said, "No, not a one."

"Then prove it by telling me about yourself as I asked you to. Start at the beginning; I want to know everything," he commanded.

The last thing Erin wanted was for him to know *anything* about her. He was disturbing and frightening and she was in constant terror of saying the wrong thing. The less he knew about the whole Brady clan, the safer they were, she decided, but he was relentless. She tried to talk in generalities, but he asked such probing questions that, before she knew it, Erin realized she had told him much more than she had intended, including her thwarted dreams of a college degree and a future in art.

"Have you thought of a scholarship?" he asked.

She shook her head. "Even if it paid all of my tuition, it wouldn't be enough. I have to work. Bob doesn't make enough to support both of us and—"

she broke off in dismay, afraid of how critical that must sound to this man who was her brother's boss.

He reached out and took her slim fingers in his warm hand, squeezing them lightly. "I'm glad to see you forgot for a moment who I am. That means we're making progress."

"I wasn't complaining, honestly," she told him earnestly. "Bob loves his job, and I'm sure he has a bright future at DSL."

"It isn't Bob's future I'm interested in right now, it's yours. I'm on the board of several foundations that make student loans. Let me give it some thought."

"Oh, no, please don't!" Erin cried. She didn't want to be obligated to this man of all people! It wouldn't work, anyhow. What she had told him was the truth. Bob's salary wasn't enough to keep up the household even if he didn't have such expensive tastes and ambitions of his own. "I'll manage to save up the money myself, and some day I'll go back to college. So please, don't even think about it."

He looked at her quizzically. "What you're saying is, you don't want anything from me. Is that it?"

"But I really appreciate your offer," she assured him, anxious not to offend. "It was very kind."

"I do believe this is the first time this ever happened to me," he said thoughtfully.

Erin couldn't tell from his tone of voice whether he was annoyed with her or not, so it was with great relief that she noticed they were approaching Aunt Ellen's house.

"There it is, that little green bungalow over there," she told him. The car pulled up to the curb and she slid over to the door saying, "Thank you so much for the ride. Please don't bother to get out."

She had intended to slip away hastily, but nothing

in this foreign car worked like any car she had ever seen. She couldn't find the door handle. Feeling like a fool, she fumbled with all the chrome gadgets, unable to find the right one.

He made no move to help her. Instead, he watched her frantic efforts with growing amusement. "What time shall I pick you up?"

"Oh, that won't be necessary," she assured him. "I'll get a lift home."

"I didn't mean tonight. I meant tomorrow night."

"I—I don't understand."

"I'm asking you to have dinner with me."

"Oh, no!" she blurted out without thinking.

He looked at her derisively. "You make it sound like a fate worse than death."

"I'm sorry," she apologized, "it's just that . . . I don't think it would be a very good idea."

"Why is that?"

"Well . . . Bob and I both work for you, and I think our relationship should be limited strictly to business."

"Do you mean I have to fire both of you in order to get a date?"

Erin gasped. He looked and sounded perfectly serious, and the moonlight striking the sharp planes of his face gave him a determined, almost predatory look. Would he actually go that far to get what he wanted? What a mess she had made of this whole night!

"You wouldn't really do that, would you?" she whispered fearfully.

He frowned and said, "Of course not, you little idiot. Is that your opinion of me?"

She ducked her head without answering. He slid one arm along the back of her seat and leaned close to her. Lifting her chin with his other hand, he examined her face until she felt her cheeks grow pink. The light was too dim for him to see, but she was afraid he could feel their warmth.

When his gaze grew too searching for comfort, her eyelashes drooped and she murmured, "I have to go, my aunt is waiting."

For just a moment his warm, lithe body pressed against hers and she caught her breath, but he was merely leaning across her to unlock the door. She felt like a small bird unexpectedly released from a cage. Before she could take flight, his lips brushed her cheek lightly and he said, "Merry Christmas, little Erin."

Chapter Two

Her first day back at work after the Christmas holidays found Erin tense and jittery, worried about how to act if she should happen to run into Jason. Which was all nonsense, of course. For one thing, the main office was rarely graced with his presence. If he should happen to walk through, he probably wouldn't even recognize her. No, it was safe to assume that he had forgotten her completely the minute she got out of the car. That little peck on the cheek certainly didn't mean anything. Nor did she want it to. He was a terrible man, and the less she had to do with him, the better. Why was she wasting time even thinking about him? Angrily banging the desk drawer shut, she started to take the cover off her typewriter.

"Hi, Erin, did you have a nice holiday?" It was Terry, who perched herself on the edge of the desk ready for a chat.

"Yes, fine, thank you." Erin's answer was purposely noncommittal, but the other girl was too preoccupied to notice. She was almost bursting with excitement.

"Have you heard the news?"

Erin shook her head. "I just got in. What news?"

"Helen Demarest is gone!"

"What do you mean, gone?" Erin asked cautiously.

"Well, the official story is that she's taking some extra vacation time because her grandmother's sick, but I hear there's a lot more to it than that."

Melissa joined them, asking, "What are you two talking about?"

"I was just telling Erin about Helen."

"I wonder if it's true—that she's going to have a baby, I mean?" Melissa asked.

"Oh, no!" Erin's exclamation reflected the dismay she felt that the gossip had already begun, but the women took it as a natural reaction.

"That's the story that's going around." Terry's eyes took on a speculative glint. "I wonder who the father is?"

"Don't you know?" Erin asked without thinking.

Both women looked at her avidly. "No! Do you?"

Erin's cheeks flushed, and she hurriedly shuffled some papers aimlessly around her desk. "No, of course I don't. This is the first I've heard of it. I just thought you'd have some ideas since you've both worked with her so long. If the story is really true," she added.

"Oh, it's true, all right. Mary Gordon got it from a very reliable source."

"Now that you mention it, it's funny that none of us can make even an educated guess about the father," Terry said reflectively. "The three of us talk about everything, but Helen has always been very closemouthed. When you come right down to it, we really don't know anything about her."

"We know she's a fine, decent person," Erin said hotly, "and that's all that matters. If she's in trouble, we shouldn't add to it by discussing her behind her back."

Before the other women could respond, Mary Gordon approached and said, "Erin, what have you been up to? The boss wants to see you."

"Mr. Martin?" Erin asked.

"No, the big boss—Mr. Dimitriou. He sent word for you to get up to his office on the double."

They all looked at her, and Erin's mouth felt suddenly dry. What could he possibly want with her? Did it have anything to do with that awful party? Or, worse yet, did he think she had started the rumors about Helen? Before she was obliged to answer the questions that threatened to break over her like a torrent, Erin grabbed a pad and pencil and said, as though it were just a normal errand, "See you later."

But the calm she managed to display before the women threatened to desert her outside Jason's office. Pausing by the closed door, she had to wait for her heart to stop racing before she could force herself to knock softly on the heavy paneling.

"Come in! Come in!" The muffled voice sounded impatient and did nothing for her self-confidence.

Timidly, she pushed open the door and saw Jason dictating into a machine, his desk piled high. He was frowning in concentration and waved an imperious hand at her, indicating that she should sit down. Erin perched uneasily on the edge of the chair farthest away, wondering what unpleasant surprise lay in store.

When he had finished dictating, he turned and looked at her. "Good morning, Erin, it's nice to see you again." His tone was pleasant enough but very businesslike. There was none of the soft teasing quality that had been present the last time she saw him. Nor was there any personal interest in that impenetrable gaze.

"Good morning, Mr. Dimitriou," she answered nervously.

For just a moment something flickered in his eyes, but he merely said, "I suppose you're wondering why I sent for you."

"Yes, I am," she managed.

"As you undoubtedly know by now, Helen, my secretary, will be gone for a while." His face hardened and he swung his chair around abruptly to gaze out the window, presenting Erin with the back of his head poised above wide shoulders in a well-tailored suit. "I've decided that you will take over her job," he told her casually.

"You can't be serious," Erin cried, jumping to her feet.

He turned back to face her, and there was a mocking twist to his mouth as he said, "I assure you I am."

"But why me?" she asked incredulously. "I'm the newest woman here. Surely it should go to someone with more seniority."

His eyes were steady on her face. "These are special circumstances."

"But you need someone with more experience. This is my first job. My typing and shorthand . . . they're . . . I'm afraid I wouldn't satisfy you."

There was amusement in his glance as it traveled slowly over her slender young figure and lovely face. "I'll be very patient, I promise, and I'll teach you everything you have to know."

Erin's cheeks flamed along with her temper. It seemed obvious that he expected her to replace Helen in more ways than one. Well, he was due for a big surprise! For perhaps the first time in his life, one woman wasn't going to succumb to the fabled Dimitriou charm.

Standing very straight and trying to keep her voice

from trembling, she said, "Thank you very much for the opportunity but I don't want the job."

There, it was out! Would she get fired now for her impertinence? Well, no matter, it was something she had to say. After the way he had practically spelled out the duties, nothing would induce her to work for him, not even her brother.

Instead of the explosion she had expected, he leaned back in his chair, a glint of satisfaction in his eyes as if he had anticipated her reaction.

"That's precisely why I chose you."

"What do you mean?" she stammered.

"I don't know exactly how long Helen will be gone," he explained. "But whenever she wants to return, her place will be waiting. She might not be back for a period of months." He paused as though contemplating something distasteful and then resumed. "If I gave it to one of the other women and she settled in, so to speak, she might be reluctant to give up the job when Helen returns. That's why you're perfect. You don't want it in the first place."

His logical and dispassionate explanation left Erin feeling like an idiot. The only way she could have felt more foolish was if she had actually voiced her suspicions to him. But she had an uncomfortable feeling from the twinkle in his eyes that he already knew what she had been thinking. How could she have been silly enough to suppose he had any interest in her when he could take his pick of the female population? But some of her reasons for refusing the job were still valid.

"I understand now, Mr. Dimitriou, but I really don't know if I could handle the job."

"Don't worry about it, you'll do fine. By the way, your salary will be raised, of course. That should fatten your college fund—and make the position more palatable."

"That's . . . very kind of you," she faltered.

"Forget it. Now go empty out your desk or whatever you have to do and get back here in a hurry. We have a lot of work to do."

Without quite understanding how it had all happened so fast, Erin found herself on the other side of the door, the hesitant recipient of a new challenge. She had a feeling there were many pitfalls ahead, and the first was explaining the situation to the other women. Were they going to resent what they must surely consider to be her good fortune? And how about Bob? What would he think of the whole thing?

As it happened, their reactions were exactly what she had expected. There were many speculative eyes in the steno pool, and, although they all offered congratulations, Erin could feel their resentment. Even when she explained that it was a temporary job, it didn't help.

Bob, of course, was delighted.

"Say, that's really great," he said enthusiastically. "Talk about having a friend at court! I guess I knew what I was doing when I brought you into the company. Between the two of us, we'll be running the place in no time."

"I wouldn't count on it," she advised dryly. "I have the feeling no one has any influence over that man."

And from what Erin saw during the ensuing days, she was correct in her surmise. Jason was the final word on any decision big or small. The three telephones on his desk provided instant communication with people all over the world, and regular conferences held in the handsome board room down the hall kept him informed on local matters.

Erin usually attended these meetings to take notes, and she was always nervous about it. Sometimes they talked so fast that her high-school shorthand was barely adequate. It was then she saw a side of him she hadn't known existed.

Without seeming to glance at her or even be aware of her presence, he would notice that she was having difficulty and say, "Okay, slow down, fellows. This woman isn't a machine, you know."

But just when she was beginning to think he might be human after all, something occurred to reaffirm her original opinion of him. It happened during one of those board meetings and concerned an employee. One of the managers in the cruise line division had been caught accepting kickbacks from a local meat packer. In order to sell to DSL, the Dawson Meat Packing Company had been quietly paying the man a bribe every month.

Erin thought she had seen Jason angry before, but it had been just a pallid imitation of the monumental rage he was in now as he said, "Fire him! I mean now, this instant! Get him out of here."

"But boss, he's been with us five years. Don't you think—"

"You heard me," Jason interrupted, eyes blazing and mouth a grim line. "I said get rid of him."

"Maybe you could talk to him first—you know, see if he has any explanation," one of the other men interjected nervously. "I'm not trying to defend what he did, but perhaps there were extenuating circumstances. . . ." His voice trailed off before the contemptuous look on his boss's face.

"What do you consider a good excuse for stealing?" Jason asked in a conversational tone of voice, although his eyes were hard and watchful.

"Well, of course there's no excuse," the man said lamely. "I just meant that maybe he was in trouble or something."

"He could have come to me if he was in trouble. I would have done everything I could to help him out.

No, he's a liar and a thief, and I find that contemptible. The matter is closed. Let's get on with business."

Erin sat quietly through the exchange, but she was appalled. True, the man was everything he said, but she was shocked at Jason's implacable fury. Not even to listen to a possible explanation. Anyone could make a mistake—except when they worked for Jason Dimitriou. In business he demanded the highest ethics; too bad his personal morals weren't as good, she thought bitterly.

It was noon of the same day when he came out of his office and leaned against her desk, reading some reports.

She continued with her typing, deliberately ignoring him. When he casually asked, "Where would you like to have lunch?" all the keys on the typewriter jammed.

The nerve of the man, not even asking her. He just took it for granted that she would jump at the chance.

Angrily, she looked up and met his calm gaze. "I'm sorry, Mr. Dimitriou. I told you I don't believe in mixing my business and social lives."

"First, could you manage to call me Jason? I know I'm a great deal older than you, but I always feel like you're addressing my grandfather, who would have asked you to call him by his first name, too. He liked pretty women. Said they kept him young," he added with amusement.

So it's an inherited trait, Erin thought, pointedly saying nothing.

"Secondly, my offer of lunch was a purely business proposal. I want you to help me pick out a present for a lady," he told her.

"And you consider that business?" she asked tartly.

"Certainly. Helen always did it."

"In that case, I'd be glad to do your shopping if that's part of my job, but it needn't entail lunch. Just tell me how much you want to spend."

"Contrary to what you think, I'm not the kind of man who delegates his secretary to select anonymous gifts," he told her severely. "I believe in the personal touch. I just want you along for a female opinion. So go comb your hair or do those mysterious things that women feel compelled to do before they can face a tuna fish sandwich."

As usual, his autocratic manner swept aside all objections. There was only one way she could get back at him. Reaching into a drawer for her purse, Erin said, "All right, I'm ready," and enjoyed his surprised look.

He took her to a restaurant she had read about but had never been to. It was dark and cozy, and they were met by a fawning headwaiter who addressed Jason by name. Looking at the linen-clad tables set with sparkling crystal and silver, Erin very much doubted there would be a tuna fish sandwich on the menu.

After they were seated and had been given huge menus with silk tassels, the waiter asked if they cared for a cocktail. Erin declined and Jason asked to see the wine list instead.

While they waited for the wine steward, Jason turned his attention to Erin, who felt curiously self-conscious. This didn't feel like a business lunch; it felt more like a date.

To cover her nervousness, she looked around the room and remarked, "This is a lovely restaurant. Bob will be terribly impressed when I tell him where I had lunch."

"You care very much for your brother, don't you?" he asked.

"Yes, we're all the family we have left," she explained. "But even when my parents were alive, he was very special to me. He was always the leader and I was the follower, maybe because there are six years difference between us. There wasn't anything I wouldn't do for Bob—still isn't, as a matter of fact."

Jason's eyes were steady on her. "And does he feel the same way about you?"

She was surprised. "Of course."

"Did he ever try to find a way for you to go to college in the winter and get a summer job?"

"No, that just wouldn't work."

"Did you ever discuss it?"

"There wasn't any point. I knew he couldn't manage the household expenses alone."

He covered her hand with his and her fingers fluttered tremulously in his grasp. "Erin, I know how much money Bob makes, remember?"

"But you don't understand. He's young, and he needs all kinds of things—clothes and a car and money to take out girls. Besides, there isn't any reason why he should have to take care of me."

"Why do I have the feeling that if things were reversed, you'd move heaven and hell to see that he could stay in school?"

Under his watchful eye, she found it difficult to deny. Maybe what he said was true, but it wasn't Bob's fault. Material things had always meant more to him. They were just different, that's all, and someone in Jason's position would never understand. She felt disloyal discussing her brother behind his back, and the feeling that Jason was critical of him made her uneasy.

Sensing that they were getting onto dangerous ground, Erin decided to change the subject. Ignoring his question, she said, "I've told you practically my whole life history, but I don't know a thing about you. Do you have any brothers or sisters?"

"No, I'm an only child."

"I always think that's a little sad," she remarked.

"You're right, it is. That's why I intend to have eight or nine children when I get married. A whole gaggle of them."

"I believe gaggle is used to describe geese."

"Then what do you call eight or nine children?"

"A very large family," she laughed.

"That's right, the larger the better," he agreed.

The wine was lulling Erin's inhibitions, and before she could stop herself, she asked, "If you feel that way, why haven't you ever married?"

As soon as the words were out of her mouth, she was horrified. But instead of taking offense, he answered, "I haven't found a young lady who would be willing to share my life-style."

Surely he could have made up a better excuse than that, Erin thought, but she merely remarked. "That seems hard to believe."

"Only because you don't really know me," he told her. "Like everyone else, you assume that all my free time is spent going to parties."

"Well, isn't it?" she challenged.

Without answering directly, he said, "Would it surprise you to know that I like to walk on the beach when it rains? Or that I'm as well known in a little family restaurant where the mama does the cooking as I am in places like this? They call me Jason there, not Mr. Dimitriou, and sometimes papa will sit down and have a glass of wine with me and we talk about life, not business or high society." He smiled at her obvious confusion and continued. "Yes, I stay at the Dorchester in London and I dine at Maxim's in Paris, but I also like to poke around in dusty old shops in out-of-the-way places. Unfortunately, the ladies I'm acquainted with don't share my enthusiasms."

This was a side of him Erin had never imagined. While she was trying to readjust her thinking, their lunch arrived.

Jason was a gracious host. When the meal was over and they walked out into the brilliant sunshine, Erin's head was in a whirl. Every time she thought she had him figured out, he revealed another facet of his complex personality. Who was the real Jason Dimitriou? Was he the callous millionaire who seduced his secretary and paid his debt with a check? The heartless tycoon who never gave anyone a second chance? Or was he, in reality, a misunderstood soul looking for true love? More probably he was just a very handsome man with a very slick line, she warned herself.

Jason's voice cut in on her speculation. "And now for the gift."

A few doors from the restaurant was a famous jewelry store that had branches all over the world. An iron gate shielded the ornate portal and a uniformed guard stood at the door, coldly eyeing passersby. His presence intimidated Erin, but Jason merely nodded at the man and the gates swung open hospitably.

Inside were thick pale rugs and a hushed atmosphere. A salesman came forward to greet them, and Jason said, "I want to buy a present for a lady—pearls, I think." He turned to Erin. "How does that sound?"

"I'm sure that would be lovely," she answered, thinking that it must be a very special lady. When he asked her help in selecting a gift, she thought he meant perfume or a purse or something like that.

Everything in this shop must cost thousands of dollars!

The salesman put down a square of midnight-blue velvet and was lifting strands of pearls out of a locked drawer. They were different sizes and lengths, but each one gleamed with a lovely inner glow.

"These are our finest quality," he said. "The difference is in your personal preference. If you will notice, some have a slight pink tint, while others are almost pure white. And these," he said, indicating some larger than the rest, "are the color of heavy cream."

"What do you think?" Jason asked Erin.

"They're all so lovely it would be hard to choose. But how do you fasten them? They only have those little threads on the end like someone forgot to finish stringing them."

The salesman smiled indulgently. "Our customers usually wish to select their own clasps," he said, reaching into another drawer and bringing out a tray of diamond, ruby and emerald fasteners, each a work of the jeweler's art."

"This diamond one is especially lovely, don't you think?"

A large center stone blazed like cold fire, and Erin was fascinated. Most women would be ecstatic to have it for an engagement ring, but in this plush establishment it was designated as a mere clasp and surrounded by other diamonds.

"It's beautiful," she agreed.

"Would you care to try on the pearls first?" he asked.

"They aren't for me," Erin informed him stiffly. "Mr. Dimitriou is buying them for . . . a friend."

The man looked from one to the other, sensing he

had made a faux pas. Jason's eyes danced with
merriment. "That's correct, and I think my . . .
friend"—he mimicked her hesitation—"would like
these. What do you think, Erin?"

He had selected the pink-tinted pearls, the ones
she would have chosen herself. To go with them,
they all decided on an intricate ruby clasp shaped
like the clustered petals of a flower.

"Then that's settled," Jason said. "Can you have
them ready for me and delivered to my office this
afternoon? I must have them for this evening."

The salesman assured him it would be done, and
Jason produced his checkbook.

Erin stood silently while the transaction was completed, unwilling to think about why he needed the
necklace that evening. Not that it made any difference to her where he was going or with whom, she
assured herself. She was merely angry at being used.

I don't know what he needed *me* for, she fumed.
He probably just wanted to show off, like a little boy
doing cartwheels to impress someone. As if I care
what kinds of presents he showers on his lady
friends!

When they reached the car, she hopped in quickly
before he could assist her. Jason smiled derisively
but made no comment as he gently closed the door.

Settling himself behind the wheel, he said, "I'll
have to tell my . . . friend what a big help you were
in selecting her gift. I'm sure she'll be grateful."

"That isn't necessary," she said coldly, turning
her head away from his mocking smile and looking
out the window.

The next morning Jason called to say he wouldn't
be in all day, and Erin banged the phone down in a
pique. The necklace must have been a success—he
had obviously had a late night! It turned out to be

one of those days when everything went wrong, and she felt cross and out of sorts. Her electric typewriter worked erratically, the phone never stopped ringing and she broke a fingernail.

About one o'clock the outer door opened and an older woman entered and made her way imperiously toward Jason's office. Erin caught only a glimpse of her carefully styled white hair and a beautiful light blue Chanel suit as she swept by.

Jumping to her feet, she said, "Just a moment. Can I help you?"

Pausing momentarily, the woman looked down her long aristocratic nose and said, "I've come to see my nephew. I am Jason's Great Aunt Harriet."

As she faced her, Erin received a shock. This woman was wearing the necklace they had picked out the day before! But why hadn't Jason told her the pearls were for his aunt? Why did he let her think—remembering the amused look on his face, she realized he had enjoyed her silent disapproval. Once again she had jumped to conclusions, and now it seemed she owed him an apology. Would she ever figure out this maddening man?

"Young lady, time is passing rapidly and I can't afford to get any older." The woman's voice brought her back to reality. "Will you please announce me to my nephew?"

"I'm so sorry," Erin gasped, "but he isn't here. He won't be in all day."

"Oh, bother! He told me to bring in some stock certificates I want him to look at, and I've just gotten them from the bank. Oh, well, you can give them to him." She handed over a large envelope. Then, noticing Erin's eyes glued to the necklace, she fingered the pearls and said, "Are you the young lady who helped select these lovelies?"

"I went with him, but he really chose them himself," Erin assured her.

The older woman smiled and immediately seemed less formidable. "I know it. Nobody makes up Jason's mind for him, but it's a good sign that he took you along. His taste in women is improving." She inspected Erin closely and, after a thorough appraisal, nodded and said, "Have him bring you to tea some day soon. You look promising. I can't stand those idle wenches he runs around with. I like a girl who has some purpose in life besides sitting around getting a suntan."

And with those words she was gone as suddenly as she had appeared, leaving Erin with her mouth open. Great Aunt Harriet was as unpredictable as her nephew, she thought, and spent the rest of the day trying to sort out her feelings.

Jason came in late the next morning. There were a dozen phone calls that had to be returned plus a mountain of paperwork needing his immediate attention. He greeted Erin impersonally, and she knew that any conversation except on business matters would have to wait. Besides, she wasn't sure exactly what to say.

It wasn't till almost noon that he called her on the intercom. Erin grabbed her notebook and went into his office. As he hung up one phone, another started to ring. Motioning her to a chair, he answered it himself. A look she couldn't quite fathom came over his face, and he swung his chair around, speaking so softly Erin could barely hear him. After a few words, he swung back to face her. "I'm sorry, this is personal. Could you come back in a few minutes?"

As Erin went back to her desk, his end of the conversation was coming over the intercom loud and clear. She had forgotten to close the key.

"I'm sorry, darling, I meant to call you, but—"
The voice on the other end of the line evidently
interrupted, and there was an edge to his voice when
he finally said, "You're being unreasonable, Marcia,
and I don't have time to argue with you right now."

Erin knew it was reprehensible to listen in on a
private conversation, and she started toward the
intercom—but very slowly.

As she reached a reluctant hand toward the off-
switch, Jason's voice was clearly audible once more.
This time the irritation in it was unmistakable. "I
never promised you anything; you knew the rules. If
you've changed your mind just say so, and we'll
forget the whole thing."

The sound of the outer door opening caused Erin
to jump guiltily. With one swift movement, she
depressed the key and turned to face the visitor.

A stunning blonde appeared in the doorway, her
long pale hair framing a beautiful yet petulant face.
The elegantly simple linen dress she wore spoke
of money, and her assured manner reinforced the
fact.

"I'm Veronica Melin. Tell Jason I'm here," she
demanded.

Her haughty attitude, as though talking to a
slightly feeble-minded servant, triggered Erin's
quick temper. She rose, intending to put this spoiled
rich woman firmly in her place. As she searched for
suitable words, a mental picture of Jason talking on
the phone to still another of his girlfriends gave her
an idea.

Smiling sweetly, she gestured toward his closed
office door. "Why don't you go right in? I'm sure he
will be delighted to see you."

Veronica swept by her, and Erin had all she could
do not to laugh out loud. She would have given a
great deal to listen in, but she didn't quite dare.

Instead, she got out some papers and busily started to type.

In what seemed a remarkably short time, Veronica came out of the office—shot out might be a better description! Although she kept on with her typing, Erin managed to steal a quick glance at the woman. She was overjoyed to see that she looked quite angry. But when Jason's door opened a few moments later, she began to have second thoughts. Having seen his temper on more than one occasion, she wondered apprehensively if she had gone too far.

He lounged casually in the doorway, arms folded and one leg crossed negligently over the other, eyeing her cynically.

"That was quite a stunt you just pulled. What was the idea of sending Veronica in without announcing her first?"

His dispassionate manner was deceptive. Erin had seen just such a calm before the storm broke, so she answered warily, "I thought you would want to see her."

"Even though you knew I was talking to another woman at the time?"

"How could I know who you were talking to?"

He didn't even bother to answer that, remarking instead in a judicious tone, "It looks very much like you wanted to cross me up with both young ladies, which is quite interesting." Looking at her with veiled amusement, he added, "If I didn't know better, I'd say you were jealous." And before she could refute those ridiculous charges, he disappeared back into his office.

Erin was so furious she almost kicked the table leg. The colossal ego of the man, thinking every female must automatically be in love with him! Was there no way to penetrate that smug conceit?

She would be glad when Helen came back, Erin

told herself. But a small voice posed a question. Would she really? In spite of the constant irritation of Jason, the job itself was interesting. She found herself looking forward to coming to work in the morning, something she never would have believed in those old days in the steno pool. Being involved in high finance was fascinating, and, as Jason's secretary, she felt a part of it. The infallible Mr. Dimitriou had made a mistake after all. Erin would be just as reluctant to relinquish her place as any of the other women. Not that she would ever let him know.

No, when the time came, she would just have to remind herself of the unpleasant aspects. And there were some. The part of her job that Erin liked least was ordering Jason's endless theater tickets and dinner reservations. She also resented having to send flowers in his name—endless boxes of long-stemmed roses and orchids and spring bouquets. It was so demeaning that she sometimes had an almost uncontrollable urge to get the cards mixed up. But remembering Jason's amused remark about her being jealous, she managed to resist the temptation. Besides, it would be dangerous to deliberately provoke him. He had laughed about Veronica, but she would never get away with it twice.

Erin saw the savage side of his nature again, but through no fault of her own. It was a call from Helen Demarest that triggered it.

Jason was out of the office when it came, so Erin took the call. "It's so nice to hear your voice. Are you having a good vacation?" she asked tactfully.

After a tiny hesitation, Helen answered, "Oh, yes, California is lovely, but it will be nice to get back."

"Well, your job is waiting for you," Erin assured

her. "Mr. Dimitriou made that perfectly clear when he asked me to fill in."

"Isn't he wonderful?" Helen asked, and Erin seethed inwardly to think that this misguided woman could still be so blind to his real character even after the way he had betrayed her. "I'm so sorry I missed him," Helen added. "Give him my love and say hello to all the women for me."

"I will," Erin assured her.

"Is there anything new around the office?" Helen seemed to want to talk.

"Nothing much, I'm afraid."

"Oh . . . well, remember me to all the women. And let's see who else. Uh . . . is Harry Martin still around?" she asked casually.

"The office manager?" Erin's voice showed surprise. Harry's domain was the general office, not the executive wing, and their paths rarely crossed. Helen couldn't really care what went on down there. She must be lonelier than Erin thought, grasping at any straw to keep the conversation going."

"Yes, Harry is still here. Do you want me to say hello for you?"

"Oh, no . . . that is . . . sure, if you happen to run across him," Helen said. "Well, I'd better hang up now."

Erin replaced the receiver slowly, feeling pity for the other woman well up inside her. She had gone along with Helen's pretense of being on vacation, but no one else had. Even though the gossip had died down after a while, it still flared up periodically. The big topic of speculation, naturally, was who the father could be.

Besides Helen, only Erin and the man involved knew the truth, and she was constantly guarding her words for fear she would inadvertently drop a clue. It was so sad. Having a baby should be the happiest time in a woman's life; instead, the poor thing was hidden away like a criminal.

By the time Jason returned in the late afternoon, Erin felt really depressed. She had a headache and her low spirits were evident, but Jason was too preoccupied to notice.

Striding purposefully toward the inner office, he called over his shoulder, "Bring your book and come in."

It wasn't till after some lengthy dictation that she had a chance to tell him about Helen's call. "She sounded fine and she asked about everybody, even Harry Martin," Erin told him, hoping to make him feel guilty over Helen's thoughtful remembrance of all the staff. But his reaction was totally unexpected.

Slamming his fist down so hard the pencils on his desk skittered, he shouted, "That slimy little toad! Don't even mention his name! I ought to—" Getting up, he shoved his chair back so violently it almost went over. Erin's lips parted in amazement, and he scowled at her, saying, "What are you sitting there for? Don't you have work to do? Get those letters out immediately!"

She gathered up her book and beat a hasty retreat, her thoughts in a turmoil. What on earth had brought that on? Was it really Harry he was angry at, or was it something else? No, the mere mention of the man had turned him into a raging tiger. He actually looked like he wanted to kill him! But if he truly hated the office manager that much, why didn't he fire him? He had never shown such self-restraint before. Maybe it had something to do with Helen. That was a thought. Did Harry know their secret and was he using it to blackmail Jason? Somehow, she couldn't imagine anyone having the temerity to attempt it, but what else could it be?

The interoffice phone rang, distracting her mo-

mentarily, and Erin received more bad news. Bob
had left a message saying he wouldn't be able to take
her home, and, glancing out the window, she saw
that a tropical storm was blowing up and she hadn't
brought an umbrella.

The whole day had gone downhill. When she
finally finished the stack of letters and put the cover
on her typewriter, Erin was glad to escape, even into
the storm. But her trials weren't over yet.

The bus stop was a long block away, and, to make
matters worse, she just missed her bus. Huddling
dejected and cold under a dripping awning, she felt
like bursting into tears. Water was trickling down her
neck and she was so sunk in misery that when a horn
blared almost in her ear, she actually jumped.
Peering through the rain, she recognized Jason's
Aston-Martin.

"Get in," he called through the partially opened
window. "I'll give you a ride home."

But she shook her head perversely. "No, thank
you."

She was already wet to the skin, and the only way
she could possibly feel worse was being cooped up in
that car with him. Maybe he had a right to yell at her
in the office, but this was after hours and she no
longer had to take it. Putting her nose in the air to
show utter disdain, she spoiled the effect by giving a
mighty sneeze.

Jason's patience was completely at an end. He
flung open the door and bellowed, "GET IN THIS
CAR!"

Erin was so startled that she did as she was told
and then wondered why. It was ridiculous the way
this man could make her do anything he wanted.

"I hope you're satisfied," she muttered. "I'm
getting your fancy upholstery all wet."

He looked at her and grinned, taking in the long

red hair, darkened by the downpour to a shade that was almost mahogany. "You look like an Irish setter that's just been for a swim. No offense," he added hastily as her blue eyes looked stormily out from star-pointed lashes.

"I don't know why you feel you have to take me home. It's out of your way, and I'm sure I'm keeping you from something more important," she said, shivering slightly in her clammy clothes.

He reached into the back seat and brought out a lap robe. "Here, put this around you."

"I don't need it," she answered primly, determined to assert herself.

In answer, Jason veered abruptly toward the curb with a screech of tires. Almost before the car stopped, he took the blanket and started wrapping it around her like a cocoon.

"What are you doing?" she protested.

"If you're too stubborn to take care of yourself, then I'll have to do it for you," he said grimly. "Do you want to catch your death of cold?" His hands were anything but gentle on her body as he tucked the robe around her.

"You don't have to treat me like a baby," she said.

"I do when you act like one," he assured her. "You've been acting like a spoiled child all week, and frankly, I'm getting tired of it."

"*I've* been acting like a child!" Erin cried. "You're the one who threw a tantrum today when I simply mentioned that Helen had asked about Harry Martin."

His knuckles were white on the steering wheel, but his voice was calm—dangerously calm—as he said, "I suggest you drop that subject right now. It doesn't concern you." But the tone of voice made it a command, not a suggestion.

"The last thing I want is to pry into your personal

affairs," she assured him. "In fact, that's my only complaint about this job."

He looked at her questioningly. "What is that supposed to mean?"

"It means there are some things I don't think are right."

"Like what?"

"I was hired as a secretary, and I dislike having to deal with your girlfriends. They call up all the time and . . . and . . . well, I don't see why I have to be the one to order all those flowers!" she ended in a burst of frustration.

Something stirred deep in his eyes and he said softly, almost to himself, "So that's what's been bothering you."

"Don't flatter yourself," she told him bitterly. "It doesn't bother me. It just takes up too much of my time."

"Since I'm paying your salary and I'm not complaining, what difference does it make?"

What he said was reasonable, which only made Erin angrier. Fortunately, they were just turning into her street, and she pointed out the house, ignoring his question.

He pulled over saying, "If you're really that unhappy with the job, you can always quit."

The temptation to take him up on it was great, if only to puncture his smug assurance. He thought she wouldn't do it—well, she would show him! But even as the angry words sprang to her lips, Erin realized how much she would miss going to the office every day. Somehow, insidiously, it had become the focal point of her life, and she couldn't give it up. But there was her pride to be salvaged, so, after a small hesitation, she said, "I wouldn't give you the satisfaction."

"What makes you think that would make me happy?" He switched off the ignition and turned to face her.

Erin struggled to free herself from the enveloping robe, but he reached out and pinned her arms to her sides, looking deeply into her eyes. "If you didn't satisfy me, I would have fired you long ago."

"I'm sure of that," she said acidly.

"It's too bad you're so sure about everything without knowing anything. Certainly not about life or love."

"And of course you're an authority," she flared. "On love, anyway."

"I know enough to go looking for it, which is more than I can say for you," he replied simply. "You're like a little china doll straight from the toy store in its original wrappings, untouched by human hands—or emotions."

Her hair was drying in the warmth of the car, and it formed a misty autumn haze like a halo around her pale face. He looked into her wide blue eyes, as turbulent now as twin ponds ruffled by a violent storm.

"You're incredibly beautiful," he said, tracing the line of her soft mouth with a gentle forefinger. "Like a sleeping beauty waiting to be awakened. Would a kiss do it?"

With a quick intake of breath, she drew back, but it was useless. His lips found hers in a lingering kiss that sent her pulses racing. How could she turn her head away when his mouth was claiming hers over and over again, draining her willpower and making her long for more? But Erin knew she had to make the effort.

"You've never been kissed like that before, have you? Is that what frightens you?" His hand stroked the nape of her neck before slipping inside her thin dress to caress first her bare shoulder, then the soft curve of her breast.

She uttered a small cry of protest and sought to free herself, but he held her easily.

"Don't struggle, my darling. Wake up and live! I won't hurt you, I promise. Let me touch you; let me teach you about paradise." His eyes were almost hypnotic, and, looking into them, she could indeed glimpse a kind of Eden.

When he drew her close, his mouth claiming hers hungrily, Erin returned his kiss with a small moan of submission. Sweet fire swept through her veins, carrying away the last of her resistance. His taut body no longer had to command her to respond; she relaxed willingly in his arms.

Her surrender produced a change in Jason. He held her tenderly now, kissing her eyelids and her temple. "My little doll," he murmured, "I waited for this so long. Sometimes I thought—but you're mine now, aren't you? I knew you would be if I was just patient with you."

The words were like a bucket of cold water in her face. It sounded like he was proclaiming a victory. But of course! Everything had gone exactly according to plan. She was just another conquest in an endless chain, and he didn't even bother to hide the fact! He was gloating because she had submitted willingly when the time was ripe. All he had to do was wait for the right moment. Oh, how could she have been such a fool? Even forewarned, she had become his prey. He was truly a pro at this sort of thing, but at least she had come to her senses in time.

With a superhuman effort born of shame and anger, she pushed him away. "I suppose you're very proud of yourself, aren't you? Well, let me tell you this—you're the most despicable man I've ever met, and I hope I'll never see you again as long as I live!"

"Erin, you don't—" He reached for her, but she eluded his grasp.

Tears of frustration filled her eyes as she flung open the car door. "And if that doesn't penetrate your colossal conceit, let me put it this way—I quit!"

Without a backward glance, Erin ran up the walk and into the small white cottage. Dimly, she heard Jason's car thunder away into the distance, the motor snarling like a thwarted animal. It barely affected the chaos in her mind. Her lips still bore the imprint of his ardent mouth, and she scrubbed at them with the back of one hand, trying to erase him from her life.

He must be the devil incarnate! For just a moment he had made her feel so cherished that she believed he really loved her. How he must be laughing right now! It didn't matter that she had come to her senses in time. He had made her melt in his arms, and that meant he had won the game. Because that's all it was to him, a battle of the sexes.

Erin was so caught up in her own agonized thoughts that she didn't even hear the sounds coming from the kitchen. Bob's voice startled her from the nightmare.

"Erin, is that you? God, I'm glad you're home! I've been going crazy waiting for you," he said.

He appeared in the small living room and she was shocked at his appearance. He looked like he had aged at least ten years since this morning.

"What's the matter?" she cried, frightened out of her own misery.

"I—I'm in a jam and I don't know where to turn. I have to talk to you about it."

"What kind of a jam?" He looked so awful that her heart contracted in terror.

Instead of answering directly, he said, "I've been all over town. I thought I could . . . well, you sure know who your friends are when you're in trouble." His tone was suddenly aggrieved.

"Bob, what is it? What's wrong?"

He buried his face in his hands, and his voice was muffled as he said, "I've been such an idiot. I don't even want to tell you about it."

"It's all right, darling. This is Erin, remember? You can tell me anything." She put her arm around his bowed shoulders and smoothed his hair, wanting to make it better, whatever it was.

He hung on to her desperately and said, "I knew I could count on you, Sis. You've always been in my corner, haven't you?"

Erin was almost in tears. "You know I'd do anything for you, Bob, but you still haven't told me what's wrong."

"I've got to raise some money right away." His voice was tense again.

"Money?" It was the farthest thing from her mind. She had been imagining all kinds of dire disasters and, for a moment, couldn't quite comprehend what money had to do with anything.

"Yes, ten thousand dollars."

Erin turned white. "You must be joking!" One look at his face told her he was serious, and that made it even worse. It might as well have been a million. "You know I don't have that kind of money —it's a fortune! What could you possibly need it for?"

He sighed and lit a cigarette with a shaking hand. "It's a long story, but I'll try to make it as short as possible. It all started at Jason's Christmas party, remember?" As if she could ever forget, Erin thought, and waited for him to go on. "I met this real cool character who was spouting off about how only peasants had to work for a living. He said the really smart people lived off their investments. We hit it off really well, and he asked me to have lunch with him and then . . . well, one thing led to another." He spread his hands out helplessly.

"But I don't understand. What does this have to do with ten thousand dollars?"

Bob looked down and examined his fingernails. "This guy told me he was making a fortune in the commodities market and asked if I wanted in on it. The way he explained it, it sounded like an absolute sure thing."

"What is the commodities market?"

"It has to do with grain and pork futures, things like that," he said vaguely. "Anyway, I scraped together a few hundred dollars." He avoided her eyes, and Erin remembered last month's rent and how she had to pay the whole thing because he said he had an unexpected expense. "At first everything was great. The market went up, and I thought I was going to make a killing."

"And then?"

"Well, then it went down, and I owed money to cover because I had bought high." Erin was having difficulty following this, but he rushed on before she could ask any questions. "I was going to sell out and take my lumps, but this guy told me not to be a chump. He said it was only a temporary thing and now was the time to plunge—really buy heavy because the market was bound to go back up. So that's what I did, but it went even lower and I was wiped out."

"But Bob, where did you get the money to do all this?"

There was anguish in his voice as he said, "Erin, you've got to believe me—I meant to put it back. I was sure the market would recover and nobody would ever know. And I swear to you that once I got my original investment back, I wasn't ever going to do it again."

Fear clutched her heart with icy fingers as she whispered, "Where did you get the money?"

He buried his head in his hands once more and his voice was tortured when he said, "I borrowed it from the office."

"How could you do that?" she cried.

"I told you I meant to return it. And I would have, too, with nobody the wiser if . . ." His trailing voice seemed to be filled more with self pity than remorse.

"No, no, I mean how could you take that much money without anyone finding out?"

"Oh . . . well, the books . . . there are ways. But that's not the point right now. The point is, you have to help me. You're the only one who can."

"What can I do? You know I don't have that kind of money."

"No, but you could talk to Jason—you know, sort of soften him up and plead for time. I think he kind of likes you. After all, he didn't make you his secretary for nothing."

Erin drew back in horror. "You're not suggesting . . ."

He grabbed her by the shoulders, giving her a little shake. "I'm your brother! Do you want to see me go to prison? He'd understand if you explained it to him, and it isn't like I'm asking for anything except a break. I swear I'll pay back every cent. I just need time."

It crossed her mind to wonder where he expected to raise that much cash, but it was all academic; she didn't think he would have a chance to try. Remembering the terrible scene over the man who was discovered taking kickbacks, Erin's eyes widened with fear for her brother. That man was lucky, he was merely fired. But Bob . . . Would Jason actually send him to prison? With a sinking heart, she knew he would.

"You've got to talk to him tomorrow," Bob was pleading, "before they actually discover it. It will look better that way."

Suddenly all her own troubles came back to her. Remembering the scene in Jason's car, she put her hand to her mouth. "Oh, Bob, I just quit my job not ten minutes ago!"

"You what?" His tone was explosive.

Erin explained the circumstances, pleading for his understanding, but he was too caught up in his own misery and fear. "You've got to apologize and ask him to take you back. It's my only chance."

The very idea was repulsive. At first she flatly refused, believing that it would be futile in any case, but Bob was desperate. He painted a graphic picture of what would happen to him, and Erin knew better than he that it was accurate. In the end, it wasn't his pleading and cajoling that turned the trick; it was the very real specter of a jail term. She agreed to go back and intercede for him, but without any real hope.

"I'll do what I can but I have a terrible feeling that Jason Dimitriou is going to extract his pound of flesh," she told Bob, not knowing how prophetic her words would be.

By the time Erin got to work the next morning, Jason was already in his office, frowning over some papers on his desk.

She stood diffidently in the doorway and he looked up, staring impassively at her. "What are you doing here? I thought you quit. Something about never wanting to see me again, wasn't it?" he remarked sarcastically.

"I—I'm sorry. If I could just speak to you for a minute."

He glanced down at the papers and said, "Perhaps I can save you the trouble. Does it have anything to do with your brother?"

The blood coursed through her pale cheeks. "You know?"

"I know," he answered, his mouth a grim line.

"Oh, but please, before you say anything, please let me explain. He didn't mean to—"

"Why are you doing the explaining? Where is Bob?" he cut in.

"He asked me to talk to you. He thought maybe—"

Again he interrupted her. "He thought he'd hide behind your skirts and maybe I'd go easier on him. Well, it won't work. You can tell that little con artist I'm going to throw the book at him and enjoy doing it. What kind of man would send a girl to do his dirty work?"

"You don't understand," she told him desperately. "He isn't really like that. It was a terrible thing to do, I'll grant you, but he isn't really bad. He's just young and impatient and he wants so much. You wouldn't know how it feels because you've always had everything you wanted. If you send Bob to jail you'll ruin his whole life, and that won't do you any good. Please—won't you let us pay you back instead?"

"Do you know how long it would take to repay ten thousand dollars?"

"I'll work for half pay," she cried, sensing a weakening. "I'll do anything you say."

He leaned back in his chair, arms crossed over his chest, regarding her insolently. "Anything?" he asked in a silken voice.

Her cheeks flamed as Jason's eyes wandered over

her slender body, sending a chill of apprehension up her spine. But she nodded her head and said in a low voice, "Yes . . . anything."

"Well, now, that's very interesting. It just might provide a whole new solution. You said that I have everything I want, but that's not true. Suppose I were to tell you I want you?"

Erin clasped her hands tightly. He couldn't be saying what it sounded like! Even *he* couldn't be so unprincipled as to take advantage of a situation that was beyond her control. Moistening her dry lips with the tip of her tongue, she waited for him to go on.

"I have a proposal to make." His eyes were watchful and told her nothing. "I have a house in Jamaica, and I'd like to take you there for a week. It's beautiful this time of year. I think you'd enjoy it—if you let yourself. How about it?"

"You mean . . . just the two of us?"

"I wasn't planning on including brother Bob," he said drily.

That made it clear enough, she thought hopelessly, her mind spinning wildly, trying to find some other answer. But looking into his predatory eyes, Erin knew she was Bob's only chance to stay out of prison. Could she possibly go through with it? He was utterly ruthless, she knew that. She had already felt his mouth crushing her lips with its urgency, but could she actually allow him to . . .

Jason got up and walked around the desk, as menacing as a falcon swooping in on his prey. He gripped her elbows lightly, sliding his hands up her arms and under the short sleeves of her blouse.

"Well, what's your answer?" He was very close, and she could almost feel the steady beat of his heart.

She put her palms against his chest in a panic and cried, "I can't!"

His hands gently massaged her shoulders as he blew a damp curl off her forehead. "You'd rather let Bob go to prison?"

"You wouldn't!" she said, but without conviction, searching his face for compassion that wasn't there.

"You know I would," he said, his arms closing inexorably around her.

Despondently, Erin gave up the struggle and leaned wearily against him. There was no other way and she knew it. He had beaten her once more. When Jason tipped her face up to his, she closed her eyes so he wouldn't see the tears in them.

Chapter Three

When the plane landed in Kingston, there was a chauffered car waiting to drive Jason and Erin to Ocho Rios, that playground of the rich on the other side of Jamaica. In spite of herself, Erin's spirits rose. This was foreign soil, after all, and she had never been outside her own country before. The British accents were intriguing and the secret patois of the natives, extremely exotic.

Navigating through the narrow streets of Kingston was an experience in itself. It was Saturday, and the flea market was in full swing. As their long limousine inched its way through the throng, Erin was fascinated by the sidewalk stands full of brightly colored merchandise and the scores of Jamaicans spilling over into the streets. At times it seemed their car would surely decimate half the population, but the crowd parted cheerfully before them and regrouped, unconcerned, as Erin assured herself by looking out the back window.

Her head swiveled from side to side in order not to miss anything. She was so absorbed in the local color that she was unaware of Jason watching her indulgently.

When they finally reached the edge of town, a new panorama spread out before her delighted eyes.

Steep wooded mountains rose up ahead as the car started down a narrow twisting road, and the dense green foliage enfolded them in a tropical jungle. Erin was enchanted until an old pickup truck rounded a curve ahead and seemed to come straight at them at high speed. A collision appeared inevitable, and she instinctively moved closer to Jason. He put a comforting arm around her as the truck rocketed back to its own side of the road at the very last minute and passed them safely with a merry beep of its horn and much laughing and waving by the native passengers.

Ashamed of her momentary panic, Erin moved away from the safety of his embrace. He made no objections, but his warm hand closed understandingly over her small clenched fist. He said, "Don't worry, it's only a little game they play. They know every inch of this road and they're really good drivers."

"They would have to be!" Erin gasped, and clung tightly to Jason's hand all the way down the hairpin-curved road.

At the bottom of the mountain, the scenery changed to picture-postcard beauty. A calm blue ocean lapped at sparkling white sands, and leafy green cocoanut palms completed the Caribbean color scheme. Here and there, a modern luxury hotel dotted the landscape, but it was mostly dominated by huge private mansions sprawled over acres of carefully tended ground. It was in front of one of these that their car stopped after traveling down a wide graveled driveway.

The long, low house was set like a jewel in the middle of lush green lawns decorated with beds of multicolored flowers, and Erin's eyes widened at the sight. In its complete seclusion, it looked like a modern pink palace, a hideaway for royalty.

While Jason helped her out of the car and the chauffeur was getting the luggage, the front door opened. It wouldn't have surprised Erin to see a uniformed footman appear, but what she actually saw surprised her even more. Lounging in the doorway with a glass in his hand was Brad Honeywell!

"Welcome, welcome. I thought you two would never get here." He saluted with his glass.

Jason reacted as though stung by a bee. His eyebrows drew together in a mighty frown and he said, "What the devil are you doing here?"

"That's a fine way to greet a good friend." Brad was all injured dignity.

For the first time since she had known him, Erin saw Jason's poise ruffled. "Why didn't you tell me you were coming?" he demanded.

"It didn't occur to me. You told me I could use the house whenever I wanted."

"Yes, but—"

"I didn't even know you were going to be here this week." Brad clearly felt himself to be the injured party. "Why didn't you mention it? Fine friend you are, having a house party without me. I had to find out from Tommy and Bibi."

"Are they here yet?" Jason asked, still scowling.

Brad glanced at Erin and took a small sip of his drink. When he finally answered, there was a peculiar smile on his face. "Yes, they're here, and they brought another guest. It's going to be a full house."

Erin was understandably confused. Although Jason hadn't exactly said as much, she had naturally assumed they were going to be alone. Seeing Brad was a surprise, but now it seemed there were going to be more people. "Who are Tommy and Bibi?" she asked.

"Tommy and Bibi Exeter, friends of mine," Jason enlightened her.

"One of the few happily married couples he knows," Brad said mockingly.

As though hearing their names, the Exeters appeared in the doorway. He was a tall, thin, sandy-haired man with an endearing, homely face, a pleasing foil for his sleek and slender dark-haired wife.

"Hi, Jason. Was your plane late?" Tommy asked. "You should have flown down with us. We've been here for hours."

"Yes, and you'll never guess who we brought with us," his wife said. "We met in the airport, and she was on her way to Bermuda. When we told her where we were going, she decided it sounded like more fun here. Isn't that nifty?" Was there a touch of irony in her voice? Bibi looked over her shoulder to include the tall blond girl who had appeared at the sound of their voices. Erin saw to her horror that it was Veronica Melin!

Something of Erin's emotion was mirrored on Jason's face as he looked at the newcomer, but Veronica seemed sure of her welcome.

Running to Jason, she threw her arms around his neck. "Are you surprised to see me, darling?"

"You have no idea," he murmured.

"It was just a stroke of luck, bumping into Bibi and Tommy that way. I ought to be very angry at you for not telling me your plans," she pouted, "but I've decided to forgive you."

"That's very generous," he said sardonically.

"Now that I'm here, we're going to have such a wonderful time, aren't we?" she purred.

Erin had never felt so out of place in her life. This whole trip was turning into even more of a nightmare than she had feared. But as she stood there trying to shrink out of sight, Jason turned and included her in the group. Although he had been thrown off balance momentarily, he now recovered his poise. As he introduced Erin to Veronica and the Exeters, anyone would have thought he had planned this whole gathering and couldn't be more pleased. Well, why not, Erin thought bitterly. He, at least, was among friends.

Veronica's greeting left no doubt about her feelings, which she didn't even bother to disguise. Eyeing Erin suspiciously, she said, "Why do you look familiar?" The implication was that of course their paths could never have crossed socially.

Erin could feel her temperature rise, but she merely said, "Perhaps you saw me in Jason's office. I work there."

Veronica took in every detail of Erin's inexpensive outfit before remarking insolently, "Of course. I remember now." Her raised eyebrows expressed incredulity. "But you call him Jason? How very strange."

"Wouldn't it be stranger yet if I called him Edgar?" Erin asked sweetly.

Brad's eyes filled with tears as he choked on his drink. Jason cleared his throat. "Why don't we all meet at the pool in half an hour? That will give us a chance to get unpacked." Putting his hand under Erin's elbow, he hurried her into the house before there was any more conversation.

Erin had time for only a glimpse of the wide, serene living room facing the ocean. Through ceiling-high windows, she saw a swimming pool glowing like a rare sapphire set in flagstone. It was an enchanting sight. At the deep end, a pair of stone dolphins spouted sparkling jets into clear water that looked cool and inviting.

She would have liked to linger, but Jason led her down a long hall to her room.

"If you don't find everything you want, ring for the maid," he said. "Her name is Rosa."

Looking around the room, Erin couldn't imagine what more she could possibly want. It was spacious and airy, and beside the large king-sized bed covered with a luxurious quilted pink spread, there was a comfortable pink and rose flowered chaise. A graceful round table stood by the window, flanked by two chairs with high curved backs painted a sparkling white.

Beyond the bedroom was a bathroom and dressing room with a mirrored, lighted table. The faucets over the deep rose-colored tub and matching sink were gold and crystal swans that looked like exquisite sculptures.

Erin was so busy drinking in all this splendor that Jason was already out of the room before she noticed the large suitcase opened on a luggage rack at the foot of the bed wasn't hers. Hurrying after him, she told him about the mistake, but he just smiled.

"It's yours. I thought you might need some things," he said.

Erin took immediate offense. Was he afraid she would disgrace him? "You needn't have bothered. I know my clothes aren't as grand as your friends wear," she told him stiffly, thinking of the chic Veronica, "but you'll just have to take me as I am."

His eyes grew cold. "I'll take you any way I like—and any time," he reminded her.

The sharp warning in his voice recalled the purpose of this trip. Erin felt a chill of apprehension. She was irrevocably committed, and he didn't intend to let her forget it. There was no one she could turn to in this house full of strangers. She felt more alone than ever before in her life.

Blinking back tears, she started to unpack. Her own unassuming things were put away in a matter of minutes. When she started on the big suitcase, Erin was fascinated in spite of herself. It contained a

complete vacation wardrobe. Evening gowns layered
in tissue paper were on top of skirts and blouses,
bathing suits and pants—everything that could possibly be needed at a plush resort.

The labels carried the names of famous designers
she had seen pictured in fashion magazines but never
hoped to own. As she lifted each garment out almost
reverently, her cheeks grew pink with excitement.
But at the very bottom was something that took the
sparkle out of her eyes. Looking like a lavender
cloud, a gossamer sheer chiffon nightgown and
peignoir set completed the collection.

Erin slowly lifted the fragile gown and looked at
the delicate lace across the bosom and the thin
ribbon straps of sensuous satin. When she held up
the matching lace robe, it felt weightless in her hands
in spite of the long full sleeves and pleated gathers
falling from the yoked back. Did anyone ever wear
something like this to sleep in? Not likely! Especially
this creation. He had included it with just one
purpose in mind. The sheer fabric would reveal
more than it concealed, the provocative clinging
folds making his male passion rise . . .

Suddenly Erin shivered in the warm room. For
one quivering moment, she pictured his hard body
covering hers. She shut her eyes so tightly that
scarlet pinpoints danced under her darkened lids.

When she opened her eyes, the sun slanted brightly
over her apprehensive face and she took a deep
breath. Why dwell on it? Tonight was a long time
away, and somewhere she would find the courage to
face it when she had to.

With her unpacking finished, Erin hurriedly
slipped into a halter-necked sea green bathing suit
that dipped lower in the front than she would have
liked. The sides were cut high, exposing a great deal
of thigh, and the whole thing could have been stuffed

into a very small pocket. Studying herself in the mirror, she had to admit it was most becoming.

A brief look at the clock told her she had been dawdling, and Erin didn't want to risk incurring Jason's wrath again. He had made it clear that she was to follow his orders—or else! Grabbing up a beach robe and slipping into a pair of sandals, she sped out to the pool.

The whole group was assembled there, but Brad was the only one swimming. Tommy and Bibi were lying indolently on wrought iron chaises covered with thick blue-flowered pads, their eyes closed. Jason was stretched out on a matching chaise across the pool from them with Veronica beside him, ostensibly occupying her own lounge but actually practically lying on top of Jason as she leaned over to whisper in his ear.

Erin hesitated uncertainly in the doorway. She was sure that Jason wouldn't welcome an interruption, and the other couple seemed to be asleep. But when Jason caught sight of her, he got up immediately, almost toppling Veronica, and came over to her.

His glance took in the new bathing suit appreciatively, but he merely said, "I'll get you a chair. Would you like something to drink?"

Erin shook her head as Brad swam over to the edge to welcome her and the Exeters opened their eyes to see what the commotion was.

"Come sit over here so we can get acquainted," Bibi called, and Jason obliged by wheeling a lounge next to her.

Bibi Exeter was looking at Erin with frank curiosity, and Erin returned the compliment. What she saw was a tall girl with a short, almost severe hairdo that managed to look just right with her high cheekbones. Bibi wasn't exactly pretty, but she had great style. Erin was to find that her generous mouth was usually curved in a smile. She and Tommy appeared to have a solid, comfortable marriage. They were constantly kidding each other and everyone else, but never with malice. Their casual acceptance put Erin at ease, and she liked them immediately.

"Have you worked for Jason long?" Bibi asked. "And how do you put up with him? He's a lamb at a party, but I've been told he's a fire-breathing dragon in the office."

"Hey, Jason, you'd better come over here and defend yourself," Tommy called. "My wife is doing a character assassination job on you."

"Nothing of the sort," she disclaimed. "I just wondered how you got this pretty girl to work for you. It must have been blackmail."

Jason's derisive smile took note of Erin's stricken face as he commented, "Something like that."

Brad heaved himself out of the pool and, pulling Erin to her feet, said, "Enough of this idle chitchat. Are you coming for a swim with me, or are you one of those sugar babies who melts when she gets near water?"

Grateful for the interruption, Erin flashed him a brilliant smile. "Certainly not. The water looks marvelous and I'd love to."

They swam the length of the pool and then played in the churning foam from the spouting dolphins. From under her wet lashes, Erin watched Jason, half expecting him to join them. He seemed perfectly content to lie next to Veronica and listen to her chatter. Every now and then he laughed out loud at something she said, and Erin tossed her head angrily and swam to the other end of the pool. It didn't make any difference to her, of course, but she couldn't understand how he could find that dim-witted blond amusing!

After a while, Brad and Erin dried off and stretched out next to the Exeters. A white-coated Jamaican man brought out a tray of tall frosty drinks, and they all relaxed in the glow of the slowly setting sun.

"Where shall we go for dinner tonight?" Tommy asked lazily.

Bibi propped herself up on one elbow. "There's a new place called the Flaming Torch. They have a floor show and dancing, and I hear the food's even good."

"Sounds great. Why don't we check with our host?" Brad called over to Jason, "Hey, chief, do you have any plans for this evening?"

Jason looked at Erin with a half-smile on his face. Noticing it, Veronica's eyes narrowed dangerously. Before she could say anything, he asked, "What did you have in mind."

"Bibi says there's a new nightclub and we thought we might try it."

"Sounds fine to me." Jason joined them and, standing next to Erin, looked down and tucked a vagrant curl behind her ear. "Is that all right with you?"

Erin might have flinched away from his proprietary touch, but she knew the simple gesture probably infuriated Veronica and was so delighted that she gave him a genuine smile. "It sounds lovely."

"That's settled, then. Is seven-thirty all right with everyone?"

They all agreed that that was fine and Veronica, who had sulkily joined them, now slipped her arm through Jason's and said, "Will you run me down to that little shopping center, darling? I forgot to bring hair spray."

"You can borrow some of mine," Bibi told her.

But Veronica shook her head, saying smoothly, "I

use a special kind." She gazed provocatively up at
Jason. "You don't mind, do you, pet?"

Jason looked at her mockingly. Erin was glad to
note that even he could see through her transparent
ruse, but he went along with her all the same. Well,
it was no concern of hers if he wanted to trail after
Veronica like a little lap dog, Erin thought bitterly.

Brad and Tommy drifted away on some errand,
and the two girls were left alone. Erin was glad,
because there was a question she wanted to ask Bibi
with no one else around.

"Are you going to get very dressed up tonight?"
she asked diffidently. Although her closet was filled
with beautiful gowns, she didn't know which one to
wear. It would be unbearable to choose the wrong
thing. Veronica would never pass up a chance to
humiliate her.

"Sure, let's shoot the works and get all gussied
up," Bibi said and then paused."If you'd like to
borrow a long gown, I have scads of them with me.
Tommy is always complaining that I pack too much
and that every porter from Caracas to California has
a hernia from toting my bags." She looked at Erin's
petite figure appraisingly. "We'd have plenty of time
to put up the hem."

"Oh, no, thank you. I have long dresses, but I
wasn't sure . . . I mean . . . well, there's no point in
pretending I'm used to this rarefied atmosphere, and
I don't want to disgrace myself."

"Don't let Veronica get to you," Bibi advised,
shrewdly guessing what was bothering Erin. "Under
those rotten manners of hers lies a really spoiled
brat, but she's not so bad when you get to know her.
It's just that she gets her tail feathers ruffled whenever there's another unattached female within five
miles of Jason."

Thinking of those patrician features and carefully

pampered body, Erin said, "She surely couldn't be worrying about me."

But Bibi shook her head disapprovingly. "Let's not have any false modesty. Have you looked in a mirror lately? If you two ever decided to have a tug of war over him, it's going to be the battle of the beauties." Looking appraisingly at Erin, she added, "But I'd put my money on you."

Erin laughed. "I never met anyone so good for my ego, Bibi. That's a really interesting name, by the way."

"It's a ridiculous name. They tell me that when I was little, I couldn't say Barbara, so I called myself Bibi and it stuck to this day. Although it's my considered opinion that society editors are responsible for perpetuating nicknames. They're afraid they'll get thrown out of the sorority if they call someone just plain Sarah or Mabel."

The two girls chattered on as if they had known each other for years, and Erin was sorry when it was time to get dressed for dinner. She felt relaxed with Bibi and was even able to pretend for a short time that this was really what it seemed—just an innocent holiday in Jamaica.

Soaking luxuriously in a perfumed tub, reality returned and she thought about Jason. Now that Veronica was here, would he transfer his attentions to her? Or would he still make Erin go through with her bargain? And if he did and they found out about it, how would she ever face the Exeters, whom she really admired? They wouldn't know she was forced into this. They would think . . .

It was too dreadful to contemplate. Getting hurriedly out of the tub, Erin toweled herself so vigorously that her delicate skin glowed.

Wrapping herself sarong style in a big towel, she went to inspect the contents of the closet. The long dresses were all so lovely that it was hard to choose, a problem she had never had before. Fingering the delicate fabrics gently, she finally selected a gown with a long-sleeved, scoop-necked top of jade-green silk jersey. The long, tulip-shaped skirt was of heavy peau de soie, and there was a wide sash to wind around her small waist, making it look even tinier. The designer might have had Erin in mind when he dreamed up this creation. With her burnished auburn hair and creamy skin, she looked as though she had just stepped off the cover of a fashion magazine. A spray of perfume provided the finishing touch.

She met Jason just outside her bedroom door. When she saw the glow in his eyes, Erin had sudden misgivings about the time she had spent making herself more than presentable. There was no mistaking the ardor on his face, even had his hands not reached out to span her waist, drawing her slowly closer.

"You look lovely." His low, caressing voice was almost like a kiss.

Surely he wasn't going to take her in his arms right here in the hallway where anyone might come along? Breathlessly, Erin put her hands against his chest and said, "Thank you, but I can't take the credit. Anyone would look good in this gorgeous gown. I had no idea that clothes could make such a difference."

The words tumbled out desperately and he smiled mockingly, recognizing the reason for her nervousness and enjoying it. "I don't think that's really true. You would look beautiful without—" He paused, and Erin flushed a deep rose, certain that he was going to say, "without anything on at all." But after a moment he continued, "—the benefit of expensive clothes."

To her great relief, a door opened down the

corridor. Jason moved casually away from her as Brad rounded the corner and joined them. After that, confusion reigned as they all assembled in the front hall and Jason turned his attention to his guests. It was decided that it would be more comfortable to take two cars. Erin didn't know exactly how it happened, but she found herself in one car with Brad and the Exeters, while Jason and Veronica were alone in the other.

That made it quite clear which one he preferred, Erin thought resentfully, and wondered why it hurt so much. She had to remind herself how much she hated this arrogant, fickle man. Besides, even if she wanted to, she could never compete with Veronica, who looked ravishing tonight in skintight turquoise silk pants and a fuschia chiffon blouse opened almost to her waist. Erin had noticed Jason and all the other men eyeing the blond woman's charms appreciatively.

When they arrived at the restaurant, Erin was almost surprised to find herself seated between Brad and Jason. She wondered cynically how Veronica allowed that to happen. But if the other woman had no control over the seating, at least she could monopolize Jason's attention. Whenever he even turned his head to look at Erin, Veronica put her hand on his arm and drew him back to her. If it hadn't been for Brad, Erin would have been left almost completely to her own devices, but he was amusing and attentive and she turned thankfully to him.

"When I decided to come to Jamaica, I had no idea it was going to turn into such a great house party," Brad told her. "I just expected to swim and sun and generally commune with nature."

Erin gave him an amused look. "Why is it that I can't quite see you as a latter-day Thoreau?"

His feelings were injured. "You're just like all the rest—you think I'm shallow and superficial."

"Not at all." She had trouble supressing a chuckle. "I'll bet you just love picnics—as long as there are no ants and the hamper is packed with caviar and champagne."

His conspiratorial grin was cheerful. "How did you know?

They laughed together, and Erin felt her troubles lifting for the moment. When he asked her to dance, she accepted with pleasure. As Brad held her chair, she glanced briefly at Jason, but he was deep in conversation with the predatory Veronica. Obviously, he didn't care what Erin did, or with whom, and her smile was a little fixed as she followed Brad onto the dance floor.

He was an excellent dancer, and following him was not only effortless but also a joy. Erin became so caught up in the intricate rhythm of a complicated number that she didn't realize the other dancers had cleared a space around them and were watching them perform. Only when the music stopped and the whole room applauded did she realize that everyone had been watching. She was consumed with embarassment.

Putting both arms around her, Brad lifted her exuberantly into the air. "You're absolutely fantastic, luv."

"Put me down," she muttered. "Everybody's looking."

"Of course they are. Let's give them an encore."

"Not on your life," she told him, and led the way back to the table.

Jason and Veronica were watching their approach with differing reactions. Veronica looked like she had just bitten into a sour pickle, but Jason's expression was enigmatic.

He rose as Erin reached the table and, helping her into her chair, said softly, "It seems you have hidden talents. Do they extend to every department?"

Erin blushed scarlet and replied, "I don't know what you mean."

"Don't you?" he murmured.

"How about this woman?" Brad asked proudly, oblivious to the byplay. "Isn't she terrific?"

"Unquestionably," Jason agreed. "Perhaps she will honor me with this dance, even though I can't promise to put her in the spotlight."

His sardonic tone caused an angry denial to spring to Erin's lips, but before she could refuse she caught a glimpse of Veronica's face. The other girl was clearly furious, and it delighted Erin so much that she accepted sweetly and even put her hand confidingly in his.

On the dance floor, she had reason to regret her moment of spite. It was a slow number, and Jason held her close, his right arm wrapped tightly around her waist, molding her tense body to his. She could feel his warm breath on her cheek, and his hard nearness caused her heart to skip a beat.

They danced in silence for a few moments and then he said, "Are you having a good time?"

"Yes, thank you," she answered, like an obedient little girl.

"You and Brad seem to be hitting it off quite well," he observed.

"That's fortunate for you, isn't it?"

He raised a questioning eyebrow. "In what way?"

"Well, since he seems to have taken an interest in me, that leaves you free to devote all your time to . . . your other guests."

"Meaning Veronica?"

"I didn't mention anyone specific," Erin said primly.

At first he was amused, but then his face sobered. "I'm sorry this week is such a foul-up, Erin. Believe me, I didn't plan it that way."

"It couldn't have turned out better if you had," she told him. "I'm enjoying Brad's company enormously."

"That wasn't exactly what I had in mind."

The look on his face should have warned her, but Erin felt a childish urge to pay him back for his neglect. "That's too bad, because I couldn't be having a better time."

His eyes were hard and the corner of his mouth quirked ironically as he tilted her chin up, far from gently. Looking meaningfully into her eyes, he said, "There are other treats in store for you that might prove even more enjoyable."

Erin drew her breath in sharply. Those ominous words made it clear that he did intend to hold her to that odious bargain. But why? It was obvious that he preferred Veronica. The only time he paid any attention to Erin was to humiliate her and remind her of how much she was in his debt.

The music ended, and Erin pulled away from him without a word, and started back to the table. Holding her head high, she tried to still her rapid breathing.

Their dinner was being served when they returned, and for a while everyone was occupied and conversation was general. Even Veronica released her proprietary grip on Jason's arm for the time being. The others commented on how delicious the food was, but Erin wasn't aware of it. She barely touched the fresh lobster cocktail and regarded the tender charcoal-broiled steak with loathing. Her nervous stomach protested with every mouthful. Would it happen tonight when they went back to the house? Jason had spelled everything out for her except the exact time, and the prospect was even more terrible now.

It was bad enough when he had caressed her lingeringly in his office and told her he wanted her. Although she had sensed his urgent male passion, there was tenderness, too. His hands had been gentle as they touched her, soothing her trembling body and evoking an unexpected response that left her shaking for a different reason.

He was an experienced lover, all right, Erin told herself bitterly. He could make a woman feel she was someone special even when common sense dictated otherwise. It was Veronica who forced Erin to face the truth. Passion and love were as far apart as the poles. It was Veronica he would marry. It was Erin with whom he would satisfy himself.

The music started again, and as she tried to swallow past the lump in her throat, Tommy leaned across the table and said, "If you're through pretending to eat, I think it's time you and I showed them what a really classy couple looks like."

Erin pushed her chair back gratefully and rose to join him on the dance floor. Any interruption of her dark thoughts was welcome, and she liked Tommy even though she didn't know him very well.

He was tall and lanky and an indifferent dancer, but she felt comfortable in his arms—it was almost like dancing with Bob. And, like her brother, he didn't beat around the bush.

"I'm not exactly sure what it is, but you look like something's bothering you. Can I help?"

She smiled at him gratefully, although unexpected tears pricked her eyelids. His concern was touching, and she felt so alone. But he was Jason's friend, after all, and her problems were strictly her own.

"Everything's just dandy," she assured him, but he wasn't convinced.

"Is it Veronica?" he asked. "I know she can be pretty hard to take, but you mustn't blame Jason. He didn't invite her here. We were the ones responsible, even though it was strictly accidental—our meeting in the airport, I mean. Of course, Bibi could have gone all day without mentioning our plans, but at least Brad isn't our fault. He just turned up like a bad penny."

Erin managed the semblance of a smile. "The more the merrier, I say. Brad is charming company, and I'm sure our host is delighted that Veronica is here."

"Don't jump to any conclusions," Tommy advised her. "I don't know how things stand between you and Jason, but I got the feeling that this was supposed to be a relaxed vacation with just the four of us knocking around this week getting to know each other. Then all of a sudden the whole thing turned into a dog and pony show."

Was that the impression he gave his best friends, Erin wondered bitterly. Just an innocent little get-together? She wondered what Tommy would think if he knew the true purpose of this holiday.

"Perhaps it isn't turning out exactly as he planned," she told him, "but I'm sure Jason isn't too unhappy about it."

He looked at her closely. "I don't think you really know Jason."

Before Erin could answer, Brad and Bibi danced up to them. With a flourish, Brad effected a change of partners.

"You're a married man," he told Tommy severely, "and you're getting much too serious with this young woman. I'm doing this in the interest of your marriage."

"You're all heart, Brad," Bibi laughed, as she twirled away in the arms of her husband.

"What was Tommy telling you?" Brad asked. "You two looked very serious."

"Did we? I can't imagine why. We were just chatting."

"No, really. Was Tommy telling you anything about me?" he urged.

"Is there something I should know?" she smiled. "Actually, I hate to hurt your feelings, but we weren't talking about you. We were talking about Jason."

For some obscure reason, he seemed relieved. "Old super wolf?" he chuckled. Inelegant but accurate, Erin thought wryly. "He's quite a guy, I can tell you that," Brad added admiringly. "We've been rivals on more than one occasion, and he always beat me out. But at least he's no competition this time. With Veronica here, the field is clear for me. She never lets him too far off the leash."

"Are they engaged?" Erin asked carefully.

"Let's just say she'd like to be, and eventually she'll wear the guy down. He just isn't ready yet."

It was what Erin had surmised, so why did she feel so suddenly bereft? They deserved each other, and it would be a shame to spoil two households!

"But why are we talking about them?" Brad complained. "You're the one I'm interested in."

His voice took on a personal note, and at first Erin was going to discourage him. But when she noticed Jason dancing with Veronica wrapped tightly around him, she tilted her head back and gave Brad a provocative look.

"Because I'm the only woman here who isn't spoken for?" she asked, fluttering her eyelashes seductively.

He held her close. "It's going to be a pleasure to make you retract those words.

With her nose mashed unromantically into his shoulder, Erin couldn't estimate the impact on

Jason. But when she finally managed to free herself slightly, she caught a glimpse of him looking at them; at least he had noticed.

She threw herself energetically into her new, if unaccustomed, role of temptress. When the music ended and they returned to the table, Brad had his arm around her waist and she was chattering animatedly with him. The others were already there and the two men stood up politely. If Erin had expected any reaction from Jason, she was disappointed. He seemed to have completely forgotten his annoyance on the dance floor.

"You look like you're enjoying yourself," he remarked pleasantly.

She forced a smile. "Oh, I am. Brad is so amusing."

"The perfect guest," he agreed before turning back to a discussion he was having with Tommy.

Erin felt snubbed by his polite dismissal. She wanted to make him as miserable as he made her, but what had made her think she could irritate him by playing up to Brad? Jason had only one interest in her, and even that wasn't any burning passion. Sometimes it seemed more like revenge.

The rest of the evening passed in a merciful blur. They drank coffee and danced and watched the floor show. Jason tried to divide his attention equally among his guests and was finally quite firm with Veronica when she tried to monopolize him. Erin wasn't fooled about his preference. She was very grateful for Brad's unabashed interest and responded more than she normally would have. Actually, his lavish attention would have been annoying at any other time. She knew better than to take him seriously, but at least he provided the semblance of an escort and kept her from feeling completely in the way.

It was late when they got home, and Bibi yawningly proclaimed that she was off to bed. Tommy went with her, and Erin was about to follow when Jason put his hand on her arm, saying to the other two, "See you in the morning—breakfast around the pool."

Veronica shot Erin a poisonous look and said to Jason, "I'm not a bit sleepy. I think I'll have a nightcap."

"Sounds good to me," Brad agreed.

But Jason's patience as a host was exhausted. "You've both had enough. It's time to turn in."

Veronica's lips parted in protest, but one look at Jason's face evidently convinced her that the evening was over. Her eyes were sullen and promised retribution, but she swept out of the room, neglecting to say goodnight as a sign of her displeasure. Brad, too, was convinced, and with a lopsided smile and a small salute, followed the angry Veronica.

"Would you like a nightcap?" Jason asked Erin.

"I thought you said we'd had enough," she commented.

"I said *they'd* had enough." He took both of her hands in a warm clasp. "We haven't had a moment alone since we got here. I'm sorry things have turned out like this."

She felt suddenly shy at being alone with him so unexpectedly but also angry and hurt. Was she supposed to feel grateful that he had sent Veronica away and was now going to give her five minutes of his valuable time?

"I'm sure everything turned out for the best," she assured him. "I couldn't have hoped to keep you entertained all by myself."

He traced her lower lip gently with his forefinger. "It depends on how hard you had tried."

She flushed at the suggestive meaning in his soft

words and said, shortly, "It's been a long day. If you'll excuse me, I'm going to bed."

A sardonic smile curved his mouth as he said, "By all means. I'll go with you."

He couldn't mean . . . Erin took a deep breath and squared her shoulders, marching down the hall ahead of him as though oblivious to his presence. Reaching her room, she put an eager hand on the doorknob, but his strong fingers covered hers, barring the way to safety. A pulse started to throb wildly at the base of her throat, and she bowed her head submissively, her whole body aware of what lay in store. Did he know that this was her first time? She had always expected to give herself with love to someone who would appreciate the gift. But not like this—oh, never like this!

Her eyes were bright with unshed tears as he turned her gently to face him. In the dimly lit hall, he seemed very large and frightening. His hands caressed her slim body lingeringly. She started to tremble and looked up at him pleadingly, but he just smiled and bent his head to hers.

She knew there was no escape by the way he drew her slowly closer, as though savoring the moment of her surrender. His lips claimed hers in a way that left no doubt about his passion. It was no longer a question of whether she could go through with it—that probing, ardent kiss declared his intentions, and there could be no struggle against his superior strength.

As Erin leaned weakly against the door, resigned and helpless, she felt a gentle caress at the very corner of her tremulous mouth. Peering shyly through her lashes, she looked into his fathomless gray eyes.

He held her chin lightly in his cupped palm and, scanning her face intently as though to memorize each feature, said with an enigmatic smile, "You'll keep." And then he was gone!

Erin's emotions were wildly mixed. Sitting on her bed in the darkness a few moments later, she tried to understand what had happened. There was absolutely no doubt in her mind that Jason had meant to possess her, but he had changed his mind. Why? Did the thought of Veronica just down the hall inhibit him? It was more likely that, given the choice, he preferred the tall, cool blond whose hauteur probably masked a passion to match his.

Erin was delighted, of course, she assured herself repeatedly. She was downright lucky to be less attractive than the other girl. But she would never, as long as she lived, understand men! Her skin still burned from the caress of those seductive fingers. How could he touch her like that? How could he kiss her in that special way when he cared nothing about her?

Was it just to humiliate her? To remind her that he could take her whenever he wanted—*if* he wanted—and there was nothing she could do about it? This would hang over her head all week, and Erin didn't know if she could bear it. She had tried to fulfill her part bravely, but this exquisite cruelty threatened to crush her spirit. She mustn't let that happen—she *wouldn't* let it! It was what he wanted!

Erin paced the room nervously, her body alive with the knowledge of him, her mind hating the reminder.

Finally, she undressed and got ready for bed, putting on one of the short cotton nighties she had brought from home. The lavender peignoir set beckoned seductively, but Erin gritted her teeth and slammed the door shut.

I'll never wear that thing and he can't make me, she vowed!

Chapter Four

The house party gathered around the pool about ten o'clock, in various stages of health. Brad was nursing a hangover, Veronica was still in a temper about last night and the Exeters and Jason were bright-eyed and bushy-tailed.

"Where's Manolo with the bacon and eggs?" Tommy asked. "I'm starving."

Brad groaned. "Could you keep it down to a low roar? And while you're at it, please don't mention eggs. Hard boiled maybe wouldn't be so bad, but why is it I picture them oozing over the plate, all ghastly yellow and white?"

"Have you ever considered leaving your liver to a medical school?" Bibi asked. "Those college boys would be impressed. I'll bet they've never seen anything like it."

"The way I feel this morning, they're welcome to it as long as they have a pickup service," Brad informed her.

"That's disgusting," Veronica told him, "and so are you. If you hadn't made such a fool of yourself last night over that little secretary of Jason's, you wouldn't be feeling so rotten this morning."

"I fail to see the connection," Brad disagreed. "Erin is my only reason for continuing on in this vale of tears." And looking around, he asked, "Where is the lissome maiden?"

"Why don't you ask Jason?" Veronica commented nastily. "He was the last one to see her."

"I think we all need some breakfast," Jason remarked smoothly. As though on cue, Manolo and Rosa wheeled out carts with orange juice and melon and steaming dishes under silver covers.

For a while conversation stopped as they all busied themselves eating—Brad gingerly, the rest heartily. When the dishes were cleared away, Jason turned to Bibi.

"I'm a little worried about Erin," he told her in a low voice. "Would you mind going in and checking on her?"

She laid a hand briefly on his arm and looked at him understandingly. "Of course. Be back in a flash."

"What would everyone like to do today?" Tommy asked.

"I don't know about the rest of you, but I planned to lie here and think beautiful thoughts," Brad answered.

"Nonsense! What you need is a couple of fast games of handball to sweat all that alcohol out of your system," Tommy told him.

Brad groaned. "You physical types are incredible. Never happy unless you're working up a sweat."

"You might try it some time," Veronica said in a pinched voice. "It's better for you than just lifting your elbow."

Brad's eyes narrowed as he looked Veronica over insolently. "My, aren't we a bundle of charm this morning? What's the matter? Jealous because you're not the prettiest girl at the party this time?"

Veronica's long scarlet nails bit into her palms as

she clenched her fists and jumped to her feet. Tommy and Jason exchanged meaningful glances, and before the irate girl could explode, Tommy said, "Hey, Veronica, how about going over to the club for some tennis? Bibi and I will stand you and Jason."

Jason put his arm lightly around her shoulders. "Sounds good to me. How about it?"

Veronica wavered for just an instant, her fury at Brad warring with Jason's powerful attraction. Predictably, Jason won out. Looking seductively up at him, she said, "I'd like that—just the four of us the way it's always been."

His eyes were expressionless, but he gave her a friendly smile and said, "You go in and change. We'll be ready when you are."

Veronica left, all smiles, pointedly ignoring Brad, who shook his head in disbelief.

"Jason, you're a wonder! How you can turn that man-eating tiger into a kitty-cat is amazing. Even when you foul up and find yourself with two dates at the same time, you manage to avert bloodshed. I thought I was slick, but I have to award you the laurel wreath. Lucky I was here this week, though, to take Erin off your hands. Even you couldn't keep up this balancing act forever."

Jason frowned. "I've been meaning to talk to you about all this attention you've been dancing on Erin—"

"No need to thank me," Brad interrupted. "Glad to do it, pal." A faint smile played around his mouth. "Now there's a really toothsome wench."

"She's a nice woman," Tommy said sharply. "She's not used to playing in your league, so leave her alone. If Jason doesn't warn her about you, I'm going to."

Brad looked from Tommy's angry face to Jason's stern one. "Why are you guys picking on me? I assure you, my intentions are strictly honorable."

Tommy snorted. "That would make it one in a row."

"No, honestly, I mean it. She's a living doll, and I think this time I'm really in love. And, what's more, I think she's fallen for me, too."

Before anyone could comment on this astounding news, Bibi returned and said to Jason, "I looked in on Erin and she's sleeping like a baby. She didn't even stir when I opened the door, and I don't think we should disturb her. Poor little kid is all tuckered out."

"Are you certain she's all right?" Jason asked with instant concern.

"Oh, sure. She just isn't used to the hectic pace you clowns insist on."

"Speaking of which, my love, we're going over to the club this morning for some tennis," Tommy told his wife. "And maybe this afternoon we'll go sailing."

In a few minutes the pool area was deserted as they all went to get their rackets. Brad changed his mind and decided to join them. His recuperative powers were enormous, but, more than that, he never wanted to be left out of anything.

The sun was already high in the heavens before Erin awoke, curiously unrefreshed. Usually she greeted each new day as a gift, so why did she feel so languid this morning? Suddenly her eyes flew open and the events of the previous day—and night—came tumbling down on her.

It had been almost dawn before she had closed her eyes in utter exhaustion, but that was no excuse for sleeping so sinfully late. Would Jason be furious? Fearfully, she looked at the clock and gasped. It was almost noon! Grabbing her robe, she raced into the bathroom and turned the shower head to a fine needle spray. After a quick shower, she toweled herself swiftly dry and ran a comb through her thick hair, trying to avoid her image in the mirror as much as possible. Those dark smudges under the eyes were a dead giveaway, and she didn't want to give Jason the satisfaction of knowing he could keep her up all night—one way or another.

Throwing her clothes on hurriedly, she grabbed up a large pair of sunglasses and rushed out to the pool area, only to find it deserted.

At first it was a letdown, keyed up as she was for a possible confrontation with Jason; but then relief set in. Rosa had told her where they had gone and relayed a message from Jason that she was to take one of the cars and join them when she got up, but she shrank from the thought. He was only being polite. He didn't really want her, and she felt too weary today to parry his barbed remarks and Veronica's spitefulness.

After declining Rosa's offer of breakfast, she decided to take a walk along the beach. It was a beautiful day, and the cool water lapping around her slim ankles felt delicious. A breeze played with her hair, unfurling it behind her like a dark red flag, and the gulls swooped overhead with raucous cries.

Erin walked along the wet sand for miles, stopping now and then to pick up an oddly shaped shell or watch a tiny crab scramble frantically back into his hole. The peace and quiet smoothed out her crumpled soul, and it was with great reluctance that she finally turned back. But something told her that she had better be there when Jason returned.

She was floating languidly in the pool when voices heralded the arrival of the house party. Erin sighed, realizing that her brief respite was over.

They straggled onto the patio, arguing noisily about a disputed call in their recent match; but Jason wasn't taking part in the discussion. He looked preoccupied until he spotted Erin in the pool. Immediately detaching himself from the others, he strolled over to the edge and stood looking down at her, his brows faintly puckered in a slight frown.

Was he angry because she had slept late? Erin looked up at him wide-eyed with apprehension. Her long hair was pinned on top of her head and the sun glinted on the tumbled curls, gilding their rich auburn with touches of copper.

"Are you all right?" he asked finally.

She nodded her head. "I'm sorry I didn't get up this morning. I . . . guess I was tired."

A smile touched his eyes, lightening his stern expression. "I understand. Did you have anything to eat?"

"I didn't want anything."

"You should have ordered a tray. You don't eat enough," he told her disapprovingly. "I didn't bring you here to starve you."

He reached out a long forefinger and made a circle on her shoulder, tracing the pattern of crystal droplets on her golden skin. His touch was feather light yet unbearably sensuous, and Erin shivered.

"Why did you bring me, Jason?" she whispered, the words forced out against her will.

"Don't you know?" he smiled, his compelling gray eyes holding hers. Erin felt shy and confused but was powerless to break their spell. In a strange way it was like lovemaking, and she didn't want him to stop.

Brad's voice brought a rude awakening, and suddenly the gates of heaven swung shut. "Hello, lazybones. It's about time you joined the party," he said, sprawling out next to them on the edge of the pool.

Erin drew a shaky breath and turned to him with a relieved smile, grateful to him for releasing her from Jason's sorcery.

"You've missed half the day," Brad told her righteously.

Erin was still unnerved, but she managed a light tone of voice. "I know, isn't it terrible? But just think how rested I'll be for tonight."

Jason straightened up abruptly and turned toward the house. Watching him go, Erin was surprised at her feeling of disappointment. It was as though a cloud had passed over the sun. What on earth was the matter with her? Why did she let this man disturb her so powerfully?

Brad was asking her a question, and she dutifully tried to focus on his trivial conversation. But part of her mind registered the fact that Veronica had come out of the house and she and Jason were laughing together near the door. Today was evidently going to be a replay of yesterday.

Erin sighed and stepped out of the pool, and Brad wrapped her in a giant beach towel, patting her dry with one end of it. He was only trying to be helpful, but she was uncomfortably aware of his hands on her body. She glanced nervously over at Jason, who seemed oblivious to both of them. Naturally, Erin thought bitterly. That bit of byplay in the pool just now was only a warmup until Veronica appeared. Tossing her head coquettishly, she looked up and smiled at Brad, who didn't notice that her teeth were clenched.

"Hi, Erin, did you have a good rest?" It was Bibi, who had gone directly to change clothes and was just now joining them.

"Yes, thank you. I'm really sorry I didn't get up with the rest of you, though."

"Don't be. All we did was play tennis, and you didn't miss anything. Brad cheats, and Tommy and Jason play for blood."

"How about Veronica?" Erin couldn't help asking.

Bibi and Brad laughed. "Veronica plays by her own rules—like she does everything else."

Delicious odors were wafting in the breeze as Manolo set up a buffet table in the poolhouse, and Erin discovered that she was hungry. One look at the delectable food on display convinced her of the fact. There was a huge platter of crabmeat salad garnished with a big scarlet claw, and a silver tray of dark green artichokes with cold curried mayonnaise to dip the leaves in. Golden wedges of mango and papaya contrasted with big scarlet strawberries and slices of the strange kiwi fruit from Australia, looking like pale green flowers with tiny black speckles forming the center. There were also hot dishes and a large fresh coconut cake for dessert. Surveying the mountain of food prepared for just six people, Erin was impressed. Everyone else seemed to take it for granted.

While they were finishing lunch, plans were discussed for the afternoon and evening, and Erin listened with growing amazement. These people worked as hard at having fun as most people did at making a living! Every detail had to be carefully orchestrated because they seemed terrified at the notion of having nothing to do. Without realizing it, Erin shook her head in disbelief, unaware that Jason was regarding her closely, a small smile playing around his mobile mouth and growing satisfaction in his eyes.

"Okay, then it's decided. We'll go sailing this afternoon," Brad said.

"But I want to get in at a reasonable hour," Veronica warned. "I have to have my hair done before the party tonight."

Erin already knew about the party. It was to be here at the house for all their friends who happened to be in Jamaica at the time, which evidently encompassed a great number of people. She dreaded the thought, since she didn't know any of them and would have nothing in common even after she met them. They appeared to spend all their time in spots like Cannes and Ibiza, or Squaw Valley and Beverly Hills. Erin knew where those places were, of course, but they were merely names in a newspaper to her. Oh, well, it was just another night, and she would get through it somehow.

They had finished eating when Manolo approached with a telephone in his hands and said a few words to Jason. But as he started to plug it into the poolhouse outlet, Jason stopped him and went into the house instead. None of the others seemed to notice, but Erin, watching his exit, wondered what girl it was this time. Her suspicions were unworthy, though. A few moments later, Manolo returned and asked if she would join Jason in the den.

Wonderingly, she followed him and found Jason sitting behind a handsome mahogany desk, busily making notes on a pad of paper. She knew immediately that it was a business call and felt instantly better for some obscure reason.

Putting his hand over the receiver, he said apologetically, "It's Dukakis in Athens, and the call is important. I meant this to be a complete vacation for you, but unfortunately this is urgent. Would you mind taking notes?"

"I'd be happy to," she assured him, and a feeling of pleasure welled up in her. This was something the exquisite but useless Veronica couldn't do for him. Besides, it felt good to be working again. The endless pursuit of pleasure wasn't for Erin.

Jason put the phone down and switched on the loudspeaker so they could both hear. She pulled a chair up to the desk. Although the den was comfortably and tastefully furnished with a printed sofa and many soft chairs, for the first time she saw that it also functioned as an office. A large filing cabinet was tucked so unobtrusively in a corner that it wasn't immediately noticeable, and she found out later that one of the deep drawers in the desk contained a pull-up typewriter.

It was a long conference and the connection was only fair. Mr. Dukakis's voice faded in and out along the crackling wire, but she managed to get everything down. If she had difficulty with a word, Jason helped her out. When he finally hung up, Erin had a feeling of satisfaction. They made a good team.

"Thanks, Erin. I really appreciate your help."

"It was nothing, I was glad to do it," she told him, meaning it sincerely.

"I feel rotten about having to ask you this, but will you type up those notes immediately? I want to get a report on this to Stevens in New York as soon as possible."

"I'll get right on it," she assured him.

"It means giving up your afternoon, but I'll make it up to you, I promise."

She had never seen him this considerate, not even with Veronica, and a warm glow suffused Erin.

"Don't worry about it," she smiled. "I find I'm not cut out for a life of leisure. I'm really happier when I'm working."

He put his hand gently on her cheek, an emotion in his eyes that she couldn't quite pinpoint. It made her feel happy and shy at the same time.

He started to say something, then evidently thought better of it. Removing his hand, he said matter of factly, "Pull the Dukakis file for me, will you? I'll tell the others to go on without us."

Erin looked up, startled. She hadn't expected him to work along with her. "You don't have to give up your sailing. I'll have everything typed up by the time you get back."

He paused in the doorway. "We must be birds of a feather. Like you, I'm happiest when I'm working. Besides, I wouldn't leave you here all alone."

Erin practically floated over to the file cabinet, her light steps muffled by the thick carpet. Opening one of the drawers, she riffled through the manila folders until she came to the *D*'s.

"Danbury, Demarest, Dillman," she murmured unconsciously to herself and then came to a sudden stop as a certain name registered. Yes, there it was: Demarest, Helen. He had a *file* on her!

Erin stared at the innocent-looking name typed neatly on the paper tab affixed to the cream-colored cardboard. It would be a breach of confidence to look inside, as she very well knew. But what kind of man documented his tawdry affairs? Would he have a file on Erin after this week? The thought made her almost physically ill! All of her previous revulsion returned, and she hated herself almost as much as she hated him. She had known from the beginning how evil he was, and still he had almost succeeded in convincing her she was wrong. Erin's breathing was rapid as she realized that she had begun to fall under the spell of this virile, handsome . . . satyr. That's how dangerous he could be!

He didn't deserve the rights of privacy accorded to decent people, and maybe there was something in the folder that would benefit Helen if she knew about it. Erin knew in her heart that that was the flimsiest of excuses, but she also knew that nothing in this world could prevent her from looking inside.

With trembling fingers, she extracted the envelope and opened it. At sight of the first page, she drew in her breath sharply. It was an adoption paper. So Helen was going to take his advice and give up the baby.

Her eyes skimmed rapidly over the legal jargon and skipped to the typed-in lines toward the bottom. Under "Mother's Name" it said Helen Demarest, but under "Father's Name" it said *Harry Martin*, not Jason Dimitriou!

Erin felt as though all of the air had been suddenly forced out of her lungs. The room spun around and she reached to steady herself on a chair. Could she believe her eyes? Everything was topsy-turvy, and she no longer trusted her own senses. Jason wasn't the father! He hadn't behaved in this vile manner of which she had secretly accused him.

How could she have been so wrong about him and why hadn't she guessed? That was the piece of the puzzle that had never made sense even while she was trying to force him into the villain's role. Instinctively, she had always known that Jason would never do anything unfair or dishonorable.

But could she be blamed for jumping to conclusions? Wasn't it logical to suppose that he was the father after that scene with Helen in his office? Thinking back, Erin remembered his words perfectly, but now their true meaning sank in. When he advised her not to let this spoil her life, what Erin took for callousness was really concern for Helen. And when he said, "Don't worry, I'll take care of everything," it was out of the goodness of his heart, not because he was in any way responsible. The depth of his concern was amply demonstrated by his raging anger at Harry Martin. The only thing she didn't understand was why he didn't fire the man. But even that answer fell into place. Helen must have asked him not to. She probably still loved the little weasel and maybe even felt that he might eventually marry her.

Having witnessed Jason's contempt for Harry, Erin realized what it must have cost to keep him on when all of his instincts were to squash him like a bug instead. She was filled with compunction at having misjudged Jason. When she realized what he was doing for Helen, in deep secrecy with no thought of any credit for it, her heart swelled with love for this complex, frustrating, exhilarating man. It was at that moment that Erin admitted to herself that she was hopelessly in love with him.

The realization didn't cause bells to peal or fire-crackers to explode in her head. Instead, it made her sad. He was so far beyond her reach that it would have been laughable if it hadn't hurt so much. This week had shown her a way of life she had only guessed at and could never fit into even if she tried. And there was Veronica, who always got everything she wanted and left no doubt that what she wanted was Jason. It amused him, but he didn't seem to mind. When he got around to it, they would un-doubtedly be married, and Erin could read about it in the newspapers. She bit her lower lip to stop its quivering.

Hearing footsteps outside the door, she hurriedly returned Helen's folder and extracted the Dukakis file instead.

"Well, that's taken care of. They're off to the yacht club, and we should have a quiet afternoon," Jason announced to Erin's back.

His voice caused a thrill of apprehension to run through her and she was afraid to turn around. Would her new knowledge show? And how about her admitted feelings toward him?

"Erin?" he asked with a rising inflection. "Is anything wrong?" She forced herself to turn around. After one look at her face, he crossed the room with rapid strides and took both of her hands in his. "My dear, what is it?"

She looked up into his concerned face, and the desire to put her arms around his neck and touch the dark hair that fell across his tanned forehead was almost uncontrollable. Something of her emotions must have shown, because his expression changed and he put his hands on her shoulders, gently bringing her unresisting body close to his. Erin's lips parted and she was enveloped in a haze of happiness until Veronica's waspish voice shattered the spell.

"I hope I'm not interrupting anything." But it was evident that's exactly what she hoped.

Jason released Erin immediately and turned to the other woman. "Of course not." After a barely perceptible pause, he added, "I thought you'd already gone."

"Obviously!" Veronica snapped.

His eyes narrowed. Ignoring her tone, he asked courteously, "Is there something I can do for you?"

She looked uncertainly from Jason to Erin and then decided that honey caught more flies. Slipping her arm through his, she said silkily, "I started to think of you slaving away in here on such a beautiful day and I decided that if I helped out, maybe we could finish up all this silly paper work and still have time to go out on the boat. Just the two of us," she added pointedly.

Erin wondered cynically what kind of help Veronica thought she could provide, since her talents seemed to lie mainly in looking beautiful, but she remained tactfully silent.

Putting his arm casually around Veronica, he led her gently but firmly to the door. "You're an angel to think of it, but there isn't anything you can do for me except go sailing and enjoy yourself. I'm sure you'll tell me all about it tonight."

The irony in his voice went unnoticed and his flattery accomplished its purpose. She left, reluctant but happy, as Erin watched contemptuously. How easy it was for him to handle his women and how stupid they were to allow themselves to be manipulated—herself included. Well, no more! There wasn't anything she could do about loving him. But love was like warts or a bad chest cold— difficult but not impossible to get rid of. She was going to work at it!

As Jason turned back to her, an eagerness in his eyes, she held the Dukakis file between them. "Here are the papers you asked for, and I'll get right to work on those notes."

One eyebrow peaked at her impersonal tone but he made no comment. He seated himself at the desk, accepting her sudden reserve with perfect equanimity, Erin observed bitterly.

The rest of the afternoon flew by as they worked compatibly with a minimum of conversation.

When Erin finished the last page, she leaned back,

massaging her stiff neck. The one thing missing in this perfectly appointed office was a proper chair for typing.

Jason's grave eyes were on her. "Are you tired?"

"No, just a little stiff," she said.

He got up and stood behind her, his strong hands starting to massage her neck and shoulders. A dangerous thrill ran through Erin at his touch and she started to get up, but he held her down impatiently.

"I'm not going to attack you, for Pete's sake. Will you just relax with me for once in your life?"

"I am relaxed," she told him distantly.

"No, you're not. You're as taut as a violin string." His long fingers stopped kneading her tired muscles and slid up her neck. Cupping her chin in his palms, he tilted her head back and forced her to look at him. "Erin, what's wrong?"

Gazing up at him from this angle, she noticed for the first time how thick his eyelashes were. Then her eyes went to his mobile mouth and she almost stopped breathing. It was an effort to remember his question. She couldn't think clearly when he was this close.

Twisting out of his grasp, Erin rose to face him, the chair putting a safe distance between them. "Nothing's wrong. I just need a little exercise. Maybe I'll go for a swim before dinner."

He accepted her answer impassively. "That sounds like a good idea. Go ahead."

As she reached the door, he stopped her. "Erin . . . thank you."

The words were simple and sincerely spoken, throwing her into even greater confusion. She wanted to answer that she would do anything for him—anytime. She wanted to say it had been pure heaven working beside him this afternoon. What she actually said was a disaster.

Trying desperately for a sophisticated note that wouldn't reveal her true feelings, she remarked airily, "Think nothing of it. That's what I'm paid for, isn't it?" and fled before the growing anger on his face.

Chapter Five

There was still an hour to go before the party started. Erin was all bathed and ready except for putting on her dress, and that was no problem. She had already selected it from the collection in the closet, and at least this time she wasn't in any doubt. It was going to be a gala affair, and the short black lace would be perfect for the occasion.

When she had first inspected it, her eyes had widened at the famous designer's name on the label. His double initials decorated all the things she yearned for and couldn't possibly afford. It probably cost more than a month's salary! The strapless top and full skirt were both decorated with a ruffle, and a black silk taffeta sash completed the outfit.

Erin inspected her slim legs critically and knew without conceit that they were very good indeed. The new shorter skirts were intended for legs like hers. In a pair of spike-heeled backless sandals, she would at least look like she belonged among all these idle rich.

A knock at the door interrupted her thoughts, and her guard came up automatically. Could it be Jason? He had looked more than just annoyed when she brushed aside his simple thank-you, and from recent experience she knew that an angry Jason was a dangerous one.

Belting the short robe more tightly around her small waist, she hesitatingly opened the door. Her fears were groundless. It was only Bibi.

"Hi, Erin. We missed you this afternoon, so I thought I'd come in for a chat. Do you have time?"

Erin breathed a soft sigh of relief. "Of course, come on in."

"It was gorgeous out on the water, and I'm furious at Jason for taking advantage of you. Imagine making you slave away on a beautiful day like this! I swear that man drops everything when he's involved in a business deal, but that's no reason for keeping you locked up in a dim office."

"I didn't mind." Erin smiled.

"But that's the point—you *should*. You have to start training these men right from the start or there's no living with them," Bibi instructed.

"Aren't you getting the cart before the horse? I work for him and *he* tells *me* what to do."

"Oh, that." Bibi dismissed Erin's job with a careless shrug of her shoulders. "I was talking about your personal relationship."

Erin inspected her fingernails carefully. "We don't have one."

"Of course not," Bibi mocked her. "He just brought you down here this week because you won the annual office typing contest."

Erin's throat felt dry, and it was with difficulty that she forced herself to say, "Something like that."

Bibi gave a little laugh. "My loving husband always tells me I'm too nosy, and I guess I am. But I like you, Erin. I'm not trying to pry into your business. I'm just attempting to give you a little advice. Tommy and I have seen Jason through a lot of love affairs, and we always breathed a sigh of relief when they were over, although I don't think any of them was ever serious. But you're different. I think you're right for him." She nodded her head positively.

Erin didn't know whether to laugh or cry. "You're really crazy, do you know that? Have you seen the way he acts around Veronica?"

"Oh, Veronica." Bibi shrugged her off. "Everyone knows she's mad about Jason, but if he really loved her he would have married her long ago. I think she's just a bad habit."

"They're the hardest to break," Erin said lightly, managing to control the quiver in her voice.

"I didn't say it would be easy," Bibi complained, "but you could at least fight for him."

Erin shook her head. "It wouldn't work. I wouldn't have a chance," she said without realizing she had made a tacit admission that she wanted one.

"Why not? You're gorgeous and you're fun and you even have brains—"

"And Veronica has the inside track," Erin interrupted.

Bibi looked thoughtful. "I don't think so."

"Well, I do," Erin answered shortly. "Have you ever noticed how he drops everything to soothe her whenever she gets in a bad mood? Which seems to be all the time," she added spitefully.

"Sure, but there's a reason for it. You don't know Veronica like the rest of us. If she doesn't get her own way, she can make the most frightful scenes, and it's really uncomfortable for everyone. Jason's the only one who can handle her. He flatters her a little bit and puts his arm around her, and that usually does the trick. But he will only stand for just so much and she knows it. I've seen him be really brutal with her, and then she toes the line for a while."

"You don't mean . . . ?" Erin's tone was shocked.

"Of course not," Bibi laughed. "Nothing physical. Jason might be a lot of rotten things, but he *is* a gentleman. You've never seen him when he's in a white-hot rage, though. He can be unbelievably sarcastic."

Erin had seen him that way, and it wasn't an experience she wanted to repeat, even though she had never been the object of it. How could a woman bear to have that pent-up anger directed against her?

"She must love him a great deal."

"Who knows if a woman like Veronica is even capable of love?" Bibi shrugged. "But she certainly has a fixation about Jason. I could bite my tongue off for telling her he was going to be here. Who knew she'd change her plans right there in the airport, for heaven's sake?"

"It wasn't your fault," Erin assured her, "and maybe it was all for the best. Since Brad showed up unexpectedly, too, at least we're an even number."

"He's another problem child," Bibi sighed.

"I don't think so," Erin disagreed. "I think he's kind of fun."

"Yes, he is fun—drunk or sober. Unfortunately, it's not always easy to tell which of those conditions he's in. But he's also the kind of man that mothers are constantly warning their daughters about."

"Are he and Jason very good friends?" Erin asked. "They must be if he's free to use the house whenever he likes."

"Jason is the most generous man in the whole world. Too many people sponge off him," she added disapprovingly, "Brad especially. As to how friendly they are—well, they went to prep school together, and I guess it's a case of old school ties, that sort of thing."

"It's kind of funny, though—Jason didn't seem to

be very happy to see him," Erin remarked thoughtfully.

"That's the understatement of the year," Bibi
grinned. "He didn't expect to see either one of them.
It was supposed to be just the four of us this
week—and that's something for you to remember.
Why do you think he asked you down here if he
wasn't interested in you?"

Erin felt herself go hot with shame and she hastily
averted her face. Bibi must never know the real
reason why Erin was here. All of her kind advice was
a waste, because Jason wasn't interested in her that
way and nothing Erin could do would change it. He
only wanted one thing from her, and it was just a
matter of time until he took it.

After all, she reminded herself wryly, he was
entitled, wasn't he? He had bought her for ten
thousand dollars, which was a very impressive sum,
even though it had to be paid back. And I'm here to
guarantee the loan, she thought bitterly.

Erin hoped at least Bibi and Tommy would never
find out. She liked them both so much. They were
warm and funny and friendly and she would like to
have known them better. But under the circumstances, the best thing that could happen would be
that she would never see them again after this
holiday. They were bound to ask about her, though
—and what would Jason say? Would he take Tommy
aside and tell him all the intimate details the way she
had heard that men do? And would Tommy relay the
information to his wife? Erin's soul shriveled inside
of her.

Bibi was getting up off the big bed where the two
women had sat cross-legged, gossiping. "What time
is it getting to be? I'd better get ready. Show me
what you're going to wear and then I have to dash."

Erin brought out the black lace dress and Bibi was

ecstatic. "It's absolutely divine and you'll look smashing in it. Jason won't have a chance tonight!"

She fingered the full skirt with the eyes of a true connoisseur and then inspected the ruffled neckline. Snapping her fingers, she said, "Got just the thing. Stay right here and don't move a muscle."

Erin was puzzled to see Bibi dash out the door, and she looked uncertainly down at the dress she was still holding. The one thing that had surprised her all week was the way the others accepted her expensive wardrobe without a question. Didn't they realize she couldn't afford clothes like these? Didn't they wonder where she got them? The only thing that might explain it was that they took such things for granted. If she had appeared in her own inexpensive outfits, that would probably have caused talk.

While these thoughts were running through her mind, Bibi reappeared with a lovely diamond pin in her hand. "Here, this will be perfect nestled in among the ruffles—very sexy and understated. Just the one jewel—don't wear anything else," she warned.

Erin stared at the glittering bauble and gasped. "Bibi, I can't wear this—those are real diamonds!"

"Of course they're real," the other girl said impatiently. "What difference does that make?"

"You just don't borrow a diamond pin."

"Why not? Diamonds don't wear out."

Erin tried again. "I couldn't possibly; it's too expensive. What if I lost it?"

"It's insured."

"That's not the point," Erin told her desperately. "I simply can't do it."

"Oh, Erin, don't be so silly!"

Bibi couldn't understand Erin's reluctance, and it took a lot of heated arguing before she finally accepted defeat. She was still shaking her head disbelievingly as she went to get dressed.

Erin was equally incredulous. The pin Bibi had offered so casually was worth a fortune! It was a stunning sunburst with a large pear shaped diamond in the center surrounded by dozens of smaller round stones. That handful of sparklers would have made all the difference in the world to Erin if she had owned it. To Bibi, it was just a decoration to be loaned on a whim. Nothing could have impressed on Erin more clearly the difference in their life-styles. She couldn't stop thinking about it all the time she was getting dressed.

There was music and laughter coming from the living room when she opened her door, and Erin realized the party had already started. She was suddenly shy and filled with reluctance. Although the mirror proclaimed that she belonged here, it was all a sham. These people would see through her instantly. Would Jason even miss her if she didn't show up? Caught in a dilemma, Erin half turned back toward her room, only to see Brad coming toward her with a broad smile on his face.

Taking her hands and holding her arms straight out from her sides, he said, "Let me look at you— you're a blooming vision of loveliness."

"You look rather handsome yourself," she smiled. Brad's deep tan was accentuated by the white dinner jacket he wore.

"We're going to be the best-looking couple at the party. The women will all be envious of you and every man will try to steal you from me, but I won't let them." Tucking her hand in the crook of his arm, he led her down the hall.

Erin didn't believe his nonsense for a minute, but she was grateful for his presence. Now she wouldn't have to walk in alone. As they reached the living room, she saw there were already about twenty people there, with more arriving every minute, as evidenced by the pealing doorbell.

It was a large room made to look even bigger, since most of the furniture had been arranged along the walls, leaving the polished parquet floor free for dancing. Through the door at the far end, more couples could be seen clustered around the red leather bar that spanned one end of the playroom. Two bartenders were dispensing drinks at top speed, and the hum of conversation was loudest in that area.

Erin saw Jason across the room at the same moment that he spotted her. As their eyes met, her heart started to thump. He looked so handsome in his evening clothes—so rugged and masculine—yet sleekly sophisticated at the same time.

Brad's voice in her ear said, "It looks like a mob scene in there, but I'll see if I can get us a couple of drinks. Be back in a minute." With a little squeeze of her hand, he departed in one direction as Jason approached from another.

There was a slight frown on Jason's face as he looked after Brad, but when he reached Erin his eyes were glowing. "You look beautiful."

"Thank you . . . I . . . it's the dress," she murmured shyly, basking in his approval.

"You said that last time. I think you're just fishing for compliments," he told her with mock severity.

The admiration on his face filled Erin with confidence and she said provocatively, "Why not? You don't give me very many."

He moved so close that she had to tilt her head to look up at him. "The way you look tonight, I think I'd give you anything you want."

Erin's pulses started to race and she was thrown into confusion. He always turned the tables on her.

Fortunately, Bibi joined them and she was spared an answer.

"Erin that dress is gorgeous, but I still think I was right about the pin." Bibi turned to Jason and said, "I wanted to loan her my diamond pin, but she turned me down cold. Isn't that crazy?"

He surveyed Erin with a lazy smile, taking in her creamy shoulders and the gentle swelling of her breasts over the low neckline. "You're right. That dress calls out for a diamond pin. If she's a very good girl, maybe I'll buy her one."

Erin could scarcely believe her ears! With a stricken look, she backed away from him. How could he humiliate her like that in front of Bibi? A man didn't offer to buy a girl diamonds for nothing. He had practically told Bibi how things stood between them, and that was unforgivable!

When he saw how his careless words had affected her, Jason groaned. "Erin, I'm sorry, it was just a joke." He reached for her cold hands and held them tightly when she would have pulled away. "I was only teasing you, little one."

His eyes were so tender as they rested on her chastened face that Erin looked at him uncertainly. She had never known Jason to apologize for anything. Had it truly been just a joke?

To Erin's great relief, Bibi evidently thought so. Glancing from one to the other, she said, "I think Tommy is looking for me," and, giving Erin an almost imperceptible wink, she disappeared.

Jason didn't even notice. His whole attention was focused on Erin, and he was struggling with some deep emotion.

"I don't know why I play these games with you," he said. "Why don't I just come right out and tell you—"

"Well, here we are and I want you to know it

wasn't easy," Brad interrupted. He was carrying two tall glasses and a couple of paper cocktail napkins. Handing one of the drinks to Erin, he said, "I hope you realize all the things I'm prepared to do for you."

A mask came down over Jason's face and the opportunity was lost. Whatever he had been going to tell her would have to wait. It probably wasn't anything important, Erin thought hopelessly.

"It looks like a fun evening," Brad commented. "I saw Dwayne and Karen in there," he nodded toward the bar. "They're always good for laughs."

"That's right," Jason agreed, tight lipped. "I'd better go say hello to them," and he left abruptly.

Veronica made her grand entrance at that point, posing for a dramatic moment in the doorway. She was clad in a long, clinging gown of silver lamé that seemed poured onto her exquisite figure. Erin looked at the other woman with a sinking heart. Wait until Jason saw that!

The room was crowded now. As people stopped to say hello to Brad, he introduced them to Erin. She was grateful to him for taking her under his wing, but she felt guilty.

"You mustn't think you have to stick by my side," she told him.

"Are you trying to get rid of me?" he demanded.

"No, of course not, but I'm sure you want to circulate and talk to your friends."

Slipping his arm through hers, he said, "We'll circulate together. I want to show you off. I want everyone to know that I have the prettiest date at the party."

"This isn't exactly a date," she objected.

"Of course it is. Whatever you and Jason have going doesn't matter right now because he's too busy anyway. Tonight you're all mine." His eyes complimented her warmly, but Erin didn't feel a thing.

Brad was a handsome man, and he was going out of his way to make her feel desirable. Why did his obvious interest leave her cold, while one kind word from Jason made her quiver like a schoolgirl? Even an angry glance from Jason was better than no attention at all. She hated this weakness in herself and vowed to put an end to it.

Giving Brad a dazzling smile, she said, "It sounds like a memorable evening."

They circled the living room and the bar, and Brad introduced her to everyone. Erin couldn't possibly keep all the names straight. She eventually stopped trying and concentrated on the conversation instead.

After she got over her initial stage fright, she found that these people were much like the ones she met in her own social circle. Some were very pleasant and others were not her type. People were people and money didn't seem to have anything to do with it. It was an interesting thought to tuck away and mull over later.

In all the excitement of making new acquaintances and moving around, she barely had time to taste her drink. Brad replenished his at regular intervals. Or perhaps he merely set them down here and there and then got a fresh one. That must be it, she decided, because he certainly didn't appear to be getting drunk.

The music started and Erin looked surreptitiously around for Jason. Would he ask her for the first dance? Although Brad had proclaimed her to be his date, wasn't she actually Jason's? She realized wryly that she was indulging in wishful thinking. As if to reinforce the fact, she glimpsed him leading a radiant Veronica onto the floor.

During the course of the evening, Erin watched

Jason out of the corner of her eye, but he never troubled his head over her. True, he was the host and had to take care of his guests, but he might have given a little thought to her, Erin thought resentfully. When he wasn't part of a laughing group, he was dancing with one or another of the attractive girls. Didn't he know any homely women, she wondered caustically.

Who needs him, anyway? Erin tossed her head and smiled brilliantly up at her current partner. She couldn't complain about being neglected by the other men, at least. Her early fears about monopolizing Brad were groundless. After the music started, it was all he could do to get a dance with her as she was whirled from one to another of the men she had just met.

"I can't get near you," he complained when the music paused briefly and he claimed her before anyone else could. "Let's go get a drink and find a quiet room where we can talk."

Erin looked at him doubtfully. "Why don't we dance instead?"

He didn't offer any argument and took her in his arms obediently, but she soon regretted the suggestion. He crushed her so uncomfortably close that it was distasteful.

Struggling to free herself, Erin asked, "How much have you had to drink?"

As though guessing her thoughts, Brad released her promptly. "Don't worry, baby, I'm not drunk. I haven't even had that much to drink." At her skeptical look, he explained, "It's my image. Everybody expects good old Brad to be the life of the party and live it up, so I don't disappoint them. I have an arrangement with the bartenders—they fill my glass with soda and just a splash of booze to color it. I stay sober and everyone else is satisfied."

Erin breathed a sigh of relief. Brad was fun and she was glad there wasn't going to be any unpleasant misunderstanding between them. When the number ended, she walked willingly with him toward the bar, only to be stopped by Tommy.

"I believe this is my dance," he said smoothly, and led her away over Brad's loud protests. "You've made quite a hit this evening; I've been watching you," Tommy commented. "Jason is apt to get jealous if you don't watch out."

Erin's smile was tinged with bitterness. "Jason doesn't even know I'm here tonight—and he cares less. He hasn't asked me to dance once."

Tommy seemed about to say something and then changed his mind. "He's been pretty busy playing host," he reminded her.

Not too busy to dance with Veronica, Erin thought, but aloud she said, "Of course. I understand and I really don't mind. Brad introduced me around, and he's been hovering over me like a guardian angel. He's really a darling."

"That's what I wanted to talk to you about." Tommy cleared his throat and then paused as though looking for the right words. "You're very young, Erin, and you don't know Brad like the rest of us do. He's a lot of fun, but he has quite a reputation as a . . . uh . . . ladies'man. He can be very charming and persuasive—especially when he's drunk."

"Oh, I know all about that," she assured him. "Brad told me."

Her answer clearly took Tommy by surprise. "What do you mean?"

"He told me all about his image and just pretending to drink." At his puzzled look, she added, "You know, the way he tells the bartenders to put hardly any liquor in his glass."

"That's a new one," Tommy snorted. "I've never heard that one before. The guy gets more inventive every day. Listen, Erin, do yourself a favor and stay away from Brad. He's bad news."

"Who's bad news?" a voice interjected, and Erin was startled to find Jason smiling down at her. As always when he was near, her pulses started to race and she felt tongue-tied; but there was no need for words. Taking her hand out of Tommy's, he swept her into his arms possessively. "It's the host's privilege to cut in," he asserted.

It was so swiftly done that she hardly realized that what she had hoped for all evening was really happening. And she hadn't engineered it. He had come looking just for her! Erin's hand rested lightly against his shoulder, feeling the muscles ripple under his dinner jacket. She was actually here in his arms! Unconsciously, she pressed her body against his hard male length and felt his muscular thighs pressed against hers. A soft sigh of pure bliss escaped her lips, and the vow to resist his dangerous attraction seemed unimportant. It didn't matter that he wasn't in love with her. Nothing mattered except the chance to be close to him like this, inhaling the wonderful masculine aroma of him.

Erin didn't know how long they danced this way. She would have been content to go on forever, but he finally broke the silence, bringing her unwillingly back to earth.

"Are you having a good time?" His deep voice caused shivers up her spine.

"Oh, yes!" Her heartfelt answer was warmer than she intended. But it was all right, since he couldn't know that he was the cause of it.

"You're the belle of the ball. I saw all the men clustered around you."

"I didn't think you noticed."

"How did you arrive at that conclusion?" he asked dryly.

"I thought you were too busy with . . . other things."

He sighed. "Erin, it would make things much easier if you would stop behaving like a child."

The blood rushed to her cheeks. He might at least have apologized for not coming near her all evening! He had plenty of time for Veronica. She raised her chin defiantly. "All I said was that you've been busy. Do you have to bite my head off?"

"I wasn't aware of doing that," he answered grimly. "Why do you always misinterpret everything I say? I was only trying to explain that I couldn't be rude to my guests."

He obviously didn't put her in that category, and Erin felt hurt and angry. "Of course not. We all know you're the perfect host." In spite of the glitter in his eyes, she continued recklessly, "Luckily, I was well taken care of. Brad saw to it that I didn't feel neglected."

The tension between them was almost tangible, and Erin could have cried. What had happened to the glorious sensation they had shared when he took her in his arms and their bodies merged? She was sure he had felt it too, but now the mood was torn like fabric on a piece of barbed wire. Why did they always fence with each other in this ugly way? Erin knew she was the one who usually started it, but she couldn't accept his polite indifference. At least when they were arguing, he knew she was alive.

Jason's face was shuttered and distant, and Erin felt chilled. She never knew what response he might have made because Manolo approached, asking for a private word.

Jason turned to her, saying with icy correctness,

"You'll have to excuse me. Shall I take you back to Brad or do you think you can find your own way?"

Fighting back angry tears, Erin raised her chin. "You don't have to worry about me, I know exactly where I'm going."

The rest of the evening was merely an ordeal to be endured. She didn't think anyone noticed a change in her, but all the fun had gone out of the party. She went through the motions of eating and dancing, laughing and talking, but it was just a charade. Jason never came near her again. Whenever she sensed he was looking at her across the room, she forced herself to appear animated, especially when she was with Brad. But if it bothered Jason, it wasn't apparent.

It was the early morning hours before the evening eventually ground to a halt. Erin was exhausted, more emotionally than physically, and she couldn't wait for it to end. Most of the guests had left, but a few diehards lingered on for a last nightcap, a last conversation about future plans. Finding herself momentarily alone, Erin felt the urgent need for a solitary breath of fresh air and managed to slip quietly out the patio door.

It was a serene tropical night and the calm elements soothed her troubled spirits. The ocean was rolling peacefully in and out as it had for a millennium, the foamy surf along the shore line touched with phosphorous as it broke on the beach. It drew her like a magnet, and she slipped off the flimsy backless sandals and walked out on the sand.

The beach was deserted, and Erin was grateful for that. But before she had gone more than a few steps, she heard muffled footsteps coming from the direction of the house. At first she was annoyed. Then, turning around, she perceived the silhouette of a tall man, obviously targeted on her, and the beat of her heart almost drowned out the ocean. Had Jason noticed her leaving? Was he coming out to put things right between them? Her hopes were fleeting as the moonlight revealed it was only Brad.

"I've been looking all over for you," he complained. "Everyone's gone and I couldn't think where you'd got to."

Erin sighed. Brad had proved to be a good friend, but she had had enough of him tonight—enough of everyone. "I just came out for a little air, and now I'm going to bed."

"Good idea. I'll go with you," he said, sliding his arms around her waist.

Surely he didn't realize how that sounded, but Erin suddenly found him distasteful. Pushing against his chest, she said sharply, "Let go of me."

For answer, he pulled her closer, nuzzling her neck and saying, "You know you don't mean that. This is what it's all been leading up to and you want it as much as I do."

"I don't know what you're talking about," she said, struggling but to no avail.

"Aw, come on, baby, this is no time to turn coy."

His mouth covered hers, and she squirmed away from the sour odor of liquor on his breath. Redoubling her efforts, she said through clenched teeth, "You're drunk! Take your hands off me!"

Instead, he started to nibble on her ear. When she jerked her head away, he transferred his passionate kisses to her neck and shoulders, sliding his mouth down to her soft cleavage. It was impossible to break his iron grip. While she was desperately trying, he hooked one leg around both of hers and threw her to the sand, falling heavily on top of her.

Looking up at his face swollen with desire, Erin was genuinely alarmed. She opened her mouth to scream, but he covered her lips with a hateful kiss. His hands were roaming over her body and she felt a terrible revulsion.

With an unexpected strength born of fear and disgust, she managed to push him over on his side. But before she could escape, he wound his legs around hers, pulling her over on top of him and pinioning her hands behind his head so her arms were around his neck. In fact, anyone who didn't know better might have thought she was embracing him. With one of his hands, he held the back of her neck in a viselike grip, gluing her face to his. The other hand was free to explore her body. Erin writhed agonizingly in an effort to get away, which only served to excite him further. He kept thrusting his body against hers.

Then, almost like a miracle, a firm hand gripped her arm and she was hauled to her feet, away from the loathsome creature on the sand. Turning to her rescuer, she saw with joy that it was Jason—but her happiness was short lived.

His face was white with fury, and, although his voice was low and controlled, the words were venomous. "Couldn't you wait until you got to your room?"

Erin gasped as though he had struck her! "You don't understand. He was—"

"I understand perfectly," he interrupted in that deadly voice. "I just find it difficult to condone your lack of . . . discretion." His look of contempt was devastating.

"Jason, I can explain. . . ." Brad had got to his feet and busied himself brushing away the sand in an attempt to avoid Jason's eye.

"Shut up and get out of here!" Each word was bitten savagely short.

Brad tried again. "Erin and I . . ." His words trailed off at the sight of Jason's face, and he hastened to do as he was told.

Erin was appalled at the interpretation being put on the ugly scene. It wasn't fair after the ordeal she had just been through. "You've got to listen to me," she cried. "It's not what you think!"

It was as though he didn't even hear her. A terrible smile curved his mouth and his eyes were cruel and mocking. "I'm surprised you two were able to restrain yourselves for the entire evening. I suppose I really should apologize for interrupting at such an inopportune moment."

She couldn't believe it! "What are you saying?"

"I'm sure you understood me." His voice was heavy with irony.

Erin was almost in tears, but she made a last desperate attempt to explain. "Why won't you believe me? Can't you see Brad is drunk? He followed me out to the beach. I had nothing to do with it."

Jason took a step closer, his hands clenching and unclenching. He made no move to touch her. "Are you trying to tell me you didn't have your arms around him? That you weren't letting him make love to you—" He interrupted himself with a derisive laugh. "What do I mean, *letting* him? You were leading the way!"

Erin's nerves were at the breaking point. She felt used and disillusioned and her anger flared to meet his, although she felt a sickness in the pit of her stomach. Naturally he was on Brad's side, as one womanizer to another. His anger was merely occasioned because someone else had tried to play with his toy. She had had enough of all of them. "Imagine whatever you like and I hope you enjoy the picture! I'm going to bed."

She started toward the house, but his hand clamped roughly onto her wrist, swinging her around. "Yes, you're going to bed, but with me, not lover boy," he snarled. "And not here. Not on the beach like two stray alley cats."

One arm went around her waist in a steel grip. Grabbing a fistful of her long hair, he savagely pulled her head back till it rested helplessly against his rock-hard shoulder. As she looked at him wide-eyed, begging for pity, his mouth came down on hers in a brutal kiss that was more like a punishment. Forcing her soft lips apart, his possessive mouth delighted in her humiliation.

In a blind panic, Erin tried to get free, but she was like a small kitten in his feral grip. He swept her up into his arms as though she were weightless, carrying her effortlessly through the house and down the hall to her room.

Kicking the door open, he slammed it shut in back of him, dumping her unceremoniously on her feet. Erin was panting as she backed away from the dangerous glitter in his eyes, but he advanced inexorably. When the foot of the bed bumped against her knees, she looked around for a means of escape, but he was on her like a tiger. With one savage motion of his hand, he tore the front of her dress to the waist.

For a moment, the only thing that registered was the enormity of the deed and she said inanely, "You've torn my dress."

"I paid for it," he snarled, "just like I've paid for you." Erin's cheeks flushed with shame, and she folded her arms over her bare breasts. He yanked them aside, saying, "Oh, no, let me see what I bought."

He pushed her back onto the bed and she lay there, looking up at him piteously, scarcely daring to breathe; but he didn't look at her face. Desire inflamed him as he gazed at her slender, defenseless body and devoured it with his eyes.

Kneeling over her, he bent to kiss the soft white skin of her stomach and when she moaned and raised a small hand in protest, he said, "No? You don't like that? Then how about this?" and placing his hands on either side of her firm young breasts, he held them together, covering them with sensuous kisses and tasting the pale pink satin circles till they turned into coral rosettes under his expert touch.

Erin had never expected it to be like this. Although she was terrified, her own body was betraying her and she was ashamed and confused. Shrinking under his hard, demanding length, she turned her face aside. This seemed to anger him more, and he grasped her chin, forcing her to look into his eyes.

"Don't turn away from me, damn it! You wanted a man—well, you've got one." His mouth explored hers with a probing passion that left her senses reeling. She uttered a small moan and clung to him, scarcely realizing what she was doing. When he finally raised his head to look down at her, his eyes were blazing. "This is what you wanted, isn't it?" When she didn't reply, the pressure of his hand increased and he said, "Answer me!"

She shook her head and whispered, "Not like this."

"You'd rather have Brad, is that it?" His strong fingers tightened around her throat, and Erin quailed before the molten anger in his eyes.

She would never convince him; it was hopeless to try. All she could hope to do was get through this nightmare somehow. There were tears in her eyes, but she called up every ounce of hidden strength and faced him bravely, terribly aware of his unleashed fury.

"I know I made a bargain—and I'll keep it. But unless you hate me a great deal, won't you let me do it with dignity?" she asked in a desolate little voice.

His expression was formidable, but he slackened his grip, never taking his eyes off her as she slipped off the bed. Erin's dress hung in tatters around her and she felt sordid, half dressed and half undressed this way. She reached in back and unzipped it, allowing the ruined gown to slither to the ground. Clad only in opaque lace topped pantyhose, her delicate contours were revealed to his ardent eyes. She looked like a lightly garbed Aphrodite rising from a sea of lace.

The silence was broken only by the sound of Jason's hoarse breathing. Erin was afraid to look at him, knowing the animal passion she would see there. She tried to hold her trembling body straight and proud, but her head drooped. Masses of tumbled auburn waves accentuated the pallor of her face, and her long eyelashes shaded dark blue eyes that were twin pools of misery.

Willing herself not to cry, she waited for the inevitable, but it didn't come. A small click alerted her raw nerves and she looked up just in time to see the bedroom door closing. The room was empty— Jason had gone!

For a long moment, Erin just stood there and stared at the door. Why had he left? What had changed his mind? Suddenly she began to shake all over with delayed reaction, and she ran to put on a robe. Shivering uncontrollably, she wrapped her arms around her body and stood indecisively in the middle of the floor. Would he be back? Somehow she knew he wouldn't.

An unbidden sensation throbbed through her awakened body as she glanced at the tumbled bed, and she buried her face in her hands, remembering her reaction to his practiced lovemaking. Although he had frightened and dominated her, he had also aroused a cascade of tempestuous emotions she had never experienced before. For a fleeting moment, she had *wanted* him to do what he was doing. Did he know that, and was he contemptuous of her for being so easy? If he only knew! No man had ever made her respond like that before, but he wouldn't believe it, Erin knew hopelessly.

Her nerves were keyed to the breaking point and sleep was impossible, but, out of habit, she prepared for bed. And all the time her thoughts were going around and around like a hamster on a wheel. Did he really believe she had allowed Brad to make love to her? Was that why he hadn't taken full possession of her once she had broken the thread of his passion? He didn't want "used goods?" She ought to be grateful, but the idea was horrible. Could she ever convince him of her innocence?

The questions went on and on as she huddled in the big bed, staring wide-eyed into the darkness. And when the morning light paled the draperies, she was no nearer to any conclusion.

Chapter Six

The next morning, Erin awoke with dark circles under her eyes and a feeling of dread as her memory returned. How could she possibly face the day? If only she could hide in this room until Jason ended her torture and allowed her to go home, but that was wishful thinking. There was no telling what he would do if she tried it. He was perfectly capable of dragging her out in her nightgown!

Some time after dawn, she had fallen into a fitful sleep. Looking listlessly at the clock, Erin had a shock—it was ten o'clock already! It would never do to miss breakfast again. Very possibly the others weren't up yet, either, since it had been quite late when the party broke up; but she didn't dare to chance it.

Splashing cold water on her face, she looked despairingly in the mirror. If eyes were truly mirrors of the soul, hers was in torment. Maybe a pair of dark glasses would hide the evidence. Pulling on a pair of white pants, she hurriedly buttoned a red silk shirt, her trembling fingers feeling like ten thumbs.

There was a murmur of voices coming from the pool. Erin forced herself in that direction, finding to her relief only Bibi and Tommy there. After greeting them, she asked cautiously where the others were.

"Veronica is getting her beauty sleep, of course, and Jason is locked up in his study working," Bibi told her. "I don't know what's eating him, but he's like a bear with a sore tooth this morning. I don't think anyone better disturb him." As Erin glanced nervously around, Bibi added, "If you're looking for Brad, he's gone." At the look of surprise on Erin's face, she elaborated. "Oh, not for good. He joined the party on Dwayne's boat for a couple of days, but he'll be back, no doubt. The wonder of it is that he could even get out of bed with the hangover he was sporting."

Erin heard the news of Brad's departure with great relief and fervently hoped that he would have the good sense to stay away until after she had gone. But Jason was a different matter. She couldn't count on him to stay locked away all day and another encounter with him right now would be too much to bear. She made a quick decision.

"Since everyone seems to be occupied, I think I'm going to do a little sightseeing," Erin said casually.

Bibi looked at her curiously. "All alone? Where were you thinking of going?"

"Oh, I don't know. Maybe into town to look around. Would you happen to know if there's a bus I could take?"

"Don't be silly! There are all kinds of cars in the garage if you want to go somewhere." The idea of anyone taking a bus was clearly eccentric behavior to Bibi. "I'll be happy to drive you if you like."

Erin shook her head. "I'm sure you want to stay with Tommy, and I'll be just fine by myself."

Bibi got up, a look of animation on her face. "No, really, Erin, that sounds like a good idea. How about it?" She turned to Tommy. "Would you like to join us in a spot of sightseeing?"

An expression of mock pain crossed his face. "To

put it succinctly, my dear wife, you must be kidding!"

"I'll bet if it was a tennis match you'd be out of your chair fast enough. Never mind, Erin, we'll have more fun without the men. I'd forgotten you've never been here before, so of course you want to see something of the island."

Erin made a token protest, but she was delighted to have Bibi's company. It would be a relief to get out of this house of cross currents for a while.

"I know exactly where we'll go," Bibi said, throwing herself into the plans with enthusiasm. "How about a trip on the Catadupa Choo Choo?" At Erin's look of incredulity, she laughed. "It's officially called the Governor's Coach, but the other is more fun, don't you think? We can catch it at the Montego Bay Railway Station, and I guarantee you're going to love it. Grab your purse and we're off." Bibi was a woman of action. Once she made up her mind, there was no shilly-shallying.

On the drive from Ocho Rios to Montego Bay, she described what they would see on the forty-mile trip into the Blue Mountains. Long before she finished, Erin was glowing with anticipation. Fortunately, when they got to the station, a train was just leaving, and they managed to scramble on board only minutes before it pulled out.

Once they started their ascent, the scenery became spectacular. It was like climbing into an emerald tunnel, a lost world where surely no explorer had ever gone before. Graceful arching breadfruit, papaya and mango trees rose above dense vegetation, and the towering cacoon vines proudly displayed their two-foot-long bean pods. This was really untamed nature in its most awesome state.

Erin's nose was pressed against the window when the jungle cleared and they pulled into a small village. It was almost a shock to discover civilization in the midst of the wilderness. A whole string of small settlements had been carved out of the encroaching forest, and their little train chugged through towns with enchanting names like Anchovy, Baclava and Porus, where smiling people took time to wave.

When they pulled into a siding at Cambridge so the Kingston Express could roar by on this small section of track the two trains shared, a cluster of gaily dressed Jamaicans was waiting to hawk their exotic wares. Bright colored baskets were artfully displayed next to polished black coral, beautifully carved wooden birds and much, much more. Huge trays of crimson mangos and ripe bananas and cocoanuts split in half to show the creamy white meat were a feast for the eyes. Erin had to be restrained from jumping out and buying everything in sight.

"Wait till we get to Catadupa," Bibi advised. "There will be plenty of time for shopping after we order our dresses."

Erin turned a bewildered face to her friend. "What dresses?"

"It's a real experience, just wait and see. You can get a custom-made dress in just a few hours."

"You're joking, of course?"

"No, really. There's this darling shop with beautiful fabrics. After you make your selection, they take your measurements and off you go. Then later in the afternoon when the train makes a stop on the way back, your dress is all finished." She laughed at Erin's look of amazement. "I know it sounds impossible, but they actually do it and the dresses are lovely."

Erin wasn't sure whether Bibi was putting her on, but when they reached Catadupa, she found it was all true. The shop Bibi led her to was crammed with so many bolts of beautiful material that the two women had trouble making up their minds. Eventually, Erin chose a satin-striped white cotton that did sensational things for her auburn hair, and Bibi decided on a sunny yellow that was equally becoming.

Then the style had to be selected, which was a major decision in itself. The two women conferred earnestly and finally settled on a simple halter-neck style for Erin, with a full gathered skirt that accentuated her tiny waist. Bibi's dress was similar except for the neckline.

After that, their measurements were carefully taken amid much laughing reassurance to a doubtful Erin that the dresses would surely be ready when they returned.

The whole project was so engrossing that they didn't realize how much time had elapsed until the shrill summons of the train startled them. It couldn't be time to leave already! Making a dash for it, they arrived on board, breathless but happy.

"That was great fun and I promise never to doubt you again," Erin said. "What's next?"

"More scenery, and then a tour through the rum factory at Magotty. We'll have lunch there. I'm starved, aren't you?"

Erin had been too excited to think about it, but she now realized that she was hungry, too. By the time they reached Magotty, both girls did ample justice to the delicious picnic lunch spread at a long table by a lovely, cool stream.

"This has been the most wonderful day," Erin told Bibi. "I can't thank you enough for coming with me."

Bibi looked at her friend thoughtfully. Erin seemed like a completely different person today.

Her eyes sparkled and her mouth was curved in a smile of pure happiness. Back at the house, she was a fragile beauty with a tentative manner that was heartbreaking. Was it Jason? And, if so, what was he doing to her? Bibi didn't know, but she was determined to find out.

"Erin, I know it's none of my business, but, as Tommy always says, that never stopped me before. I think there's something between you and Jason that's making you unhappy. Would you like to talk about it?"

Erin's radiant smile dimmed at the mention of his name and the perfect day was subtly marred. Why did Bibi have to bring her back to earth? Of course, none of the problems had gone away, but they had been safely pushed to the back of her mind. Now, through Bibi's attempt at being helpful, Erin was forced to face them again. Suddenly, Jason's image surfaced, the way she had seen him last night, with contempt blazing from his eyes. Unconsciously, Erin wrapped her arms around herself, remembering how his avid gaze had raked her almost nude body.

"I know something's gone wrong between you two," Bibi was saying, "and I feel just awful about it. Tommy and I were both hoping . . ." her voice trailed off.

Erin was touched, but it didn't change anything. There was no way she could explain that Jason had never felt anything but desire for her, and he didn't even feel that anymore. His rejection had been almost worse than his brutal passion, and she couldn't bear to experience it again. Somehow she would have to convince Bibi to give up her matchmaking.

"It's darling of you to be concerned, but really, there's never been anything serious between Jason and me," Erin said lightly. "You said yourself you've seen him through stacks of girlfriends."

"With one difference. You're the first one to get Tommy's stamp of approval, and that's not lightly given."

Erin's heart twisted inside her and she felt as if she were taking their friendship under false pretenses. Carefully brushing a small crumb off the table, she said, "I don't think Jason would let even Tommy do his choosing for him. And let's not forget Veronica."

"That's the whole problem—Brad and Veronica," Bibi said impatiently. "Those two could set a pack of angels at each other's throats. At least he had the good sense to take himself off somewhere, so now we'll just have to work at getting rid of *her*."

Bibi's manner was so determined that Erin had to laugh in spite of herself. "I don't think Veronica ever did anything in her life that she didn't want to do. You'd better give it up."

"She never could beat me at anything, even in nursery school," Bibi scoffed. "Just give me a little time."

To Erin's relief, the conversation ended there as Bibi said it was time to visit the rum factory. Although Erin was still upset by their talk, the tour proved to be as interesting as everything else on this novel trip, and she was soon fascinated by the sights and smells.

A pungent aroma hung over the huge vats and stainless steel equipment and even permeated the bottling plant, which proved to be the favorite of both women. They watched in delight as rows of bottles moved down the conveyor belt like tiny soldiers doing precise drill. Each turned at exactly the right moment to receive a cork or a label, and it was like a caricature of the Radio City Rockettes.

The women found it difficult to tear themselves

away, but the train was waiting and it was getting toward late afternoon. The return trip was shorter, since it made only one stop at Catadupa to pick up their purchases. Erin watched the scenery fly by, reluctant to see the day end.

By the time they pulled into the station and then made the drive home, it was quite late. Erin began to feel apprehensive. Would Jason be angry because she had been gone all day? Even though he couldn't stand the sight of her, he might not like the idea of her just disappearing for that long. Should she have asked his permission? She set her jaw determinedly. After all, he didn't own her! But she was very quiet as she trailed into the house after Bibi.

Jason and Veronica were alone in the bar off the living room. When the women looked in to say hello, he crossed the room with swift strides.

"Where the devil have you been all day?" he demanded.

Bibi was surprised. "Didn't Tommy tell you? We took the Catadupa Choo Choo."

He frowned. "That was this morning. You've been gone for hours."

"It's an all-day trip, and we had to drive home from Mobay," Bibi told him. "Don't tell me you were worried about us."

"You bet I was worried," he answered grimly. "Knowing the way you drive, I was about to call the local jails."

"Your concern is touching." An impish look came over her face. "Were you worried about me or Erin?"

"About Erin, naturally," he told her smoothly. "Good secretaries are hard to find, and I already have her trained."

It was said lightly, as a joke, but that about summed up his feelings, Erin thought grimly. She was supposed to jump when he commanded like a circus poodle. Turning aside to hide the sudden tears that stung her eyelids, she started for the door. But his voice stopped her.

"Did you enjoy the trip, Erin?"

She turned back fractionally, just enough to satisfy good manners. "Yes, it was very interesting."

"Tell us about it." His tone was preemptory, and Erin felt like a little child being called upon to recite for company. Why was he trying to humiliate her? Wasn't last night enough?

Veronica's petulant voice cut in. "Oh, for heaven's sake, Jason, who cares about a tourist trip on a hick train?"

"Have you ever been on it?" Bibi demanded.

"Of course not! I'd have to be tied up and kidnapped before anyone could get me on that dumb thing."

Bibi's face took on a speculative look, and she raised her eyebrows at Erin, who suddenly felt better. They both laughed and Jason, who was watching them closely, asked what was so funny.

"Just a private joke," Bibi told him airily. "Erin, let's show them the dresses we had made."

But Veronica said, "Not now. We're on our way to a cocktail party at the Detweilers."

Bibi looked to Jason for confirmation and he nodded. "Tommy is still at the club. He wanted to play singles, so we left him there. We'll wait for you to get ready and he can join us whenever he's through."

"We're late already," Veronica complained. "How long will it take you?" From the tone of her voice it was obvious that she didn't welcome their company.

"There's no big rush to get to the Detweilers," Bibi said. "Their parties last forever. I feel grubby and I'll bet Erin does, too. I'm going to soak in the tub for hours, so you and Jason go on ahead. We'll wait for Tommy."

Veronica looked like she had just been presented with a saucer of cream, and Jason didn't look too unhappy, either, Erin thought grimly. His face was expressionless, but he made no attempt to urge the two to join them. Veronica hustled him out of the house before he could have second thoughts.

"Take your time, Erin," Bibi said after they had gone. "Knowing Tommy, he won't be home for quite a while."

"If you don't mind, I think I'll stay home," Erin told her. "It's been a full day, and I'd just like to curl up with a book."

Bibi shrugged. "If that's what you feel like, why not? Are you sure?"

"Yes. I'm really not used to all this partying. I don't see how you do it every night."

"It gets to be a way of life," Bibi told her cheerfully. "Well, if you change your mind, just holler."

But as Erin ran a bath and poured fragrant bath salts into the swirling water, she knew she wouldn't change her mind. Let Veronica have her triumph. At least tonight Erin wouldn't have to watch it.

Luxuriating in the tub for a long time, Erin felt her tensions lifting as the scented water relaxed her. By the time she got out and dried herself, there were muffled voices down the hall, indicating that Tommy had returned and he and Bibi were getting ready for the party.

Sweeping her auburn hair off her neck, she pinned it carelessly on top of her head and slipped into a lightweight robe. As she reentered the bedroom, there was a knock at the door.

"Erin," Bibi called, "we're about ready to leave, but you still have time to change your mind."

Erin opened the door and smilingly shook her head. "No, thanks, you two go on." And looking at her friend resplendent in finery, she added, "You look gorgeous."

"And you look comfortable. For two pins, I'd kick off these spike heels and stay home with you."

"Nonsense! Go ahead and have fun," Erin told her.

After they had left, an eerie silence settled on the house, accustomed as it was to the ring of voices. Rosa and Manolo were somewhere about, but no sound reached Erin's bedroom and she felt completely isolated. Well, this was what she had wanted, wasn't it? She walked to the window and looked out at the calm ocean sparkling in the moonlight. Was Jason looking at it, too—with Veronica?

Turning away abruptly, she walked with determined steps to her bedside table, where a stack of books were piled. This moping around had to stop. If he thought she was going to waste her time wondering what he was doing, he had another thought coming. After much deliberation, she chose a current novel she had been wanting to read and carried it over to the chaise. Tucking her bare feet under her, she started to read, forcing herself to concentrate.

It proved to be an engrossing story, and Erin was completely oblivious to the passing time until a knock sounded at her door. Oh, dear, she thought guiltily, that was probably Rosa or Manolo wanting to know when she wanted dinner. She had completely forgotten to tell them she wasn't hungry, and now she had held them up for no good reason.

"Come in," she called, prepared to apologize.

But when the door opened, Erin received a shock. Jason stood in the doorway, tight lipped yet looking impossibly handsome. With a thudding heart, Erin scrambled to her feet, tightening the thin robe around herself more securely.

Jason noticed the unconscious gesture and a faintly derisive smile touched his mouth. He merely said, "What are you doing here?"

"Shouldn't I be asking you that?"

He frowned, ignoring her question. "I told you to come with Bibi and Tommy. Why didn't you?"

"No, you didn't," Erin said defensively. "You told Bibi to wait for Tommy. You didn't mention me. Besides, I thought you'd be pleased. This way there are two couples. No one needs an extra woman."

His expression changed and there was an unaccountable gleam in his eyes as he studied her closely. "Is that why you didn't come? Because of Veronica?"

Did he think she was jealous of that dumb blond? Erin gritted her teeth. She would correct that impression right now! Adopting an elaborately casual tone, she said, "Well, when Brad was here we made an even number, but five is kind of awkward, don't you think?"

Jason's face darkened and he took a step toward her while Erin held her breath. Mentioning Brad's name had been foolhardy, but it was the only way she could think to get back at him. Had she gone too far?

His eyes were stormy as he said shortly, "Get your clothes on. You're coming to the party."

"I'd rather not," she said.

He looked at her coldly. "I said you're coming."

Stung by his preemptory tone, Erin's anger rose to meet his. "I won't and you can't make me!"

Jason smiled, but his eyes were hard. Reaching

out almost lazily, he took the pins out of her hair. It tumbled in a silken curtain about her flushed face. He was very close to her now, and she started to tremble as his glance swept casually over her slim body. She clutched the deep vee of her robe together and then regretted the inadvertent gesture as his gaze was drawn to the soft upward thrust of her breasts under the thin fabric.

"You have two choices," he said softly. "Either you get dressed by yourself or I'll do it for you."

Erin drew her breath in sharply. There was no doubt that he meant exactly what he said, and he had left her no way to back down gracefully. But it was her own fault for challenging him directly. Hadn't she learned by now that Jason Dimitriou always came out a winner?

Her face was mutinous as she admitted defeat. "Give me a few minutes and I'll be ready." He inclined his head regally and sat down in a chair, picking up the book she had been reading. Erin looked at him in astonishment. "Aren't you going to wait outside?"

He looked up with complete disinterest. "Don't be such a child—and don't dawdle. I've wasted enough time coming all the way back here to get you, so see that you speed it up or I'll have to give you a hand."

Giving him an outraged look, she moved self-consciously to the closet and took the first dress she touched. Then, gathering up the rest of her things, she took them into the dressing room and securely locked the door. Luckily for Erin, she was spared the look of amusement on his face when he heard the latch click.

In record time, she reappeared, fully clothed but with a rebellious expression on her face, which Jason ignored. Taking her chin in his hand, he inspected her minutely and said, "You look pale. Put on some rouge."

"I don't use rouge," she told him.

"You will tonight," he assured her.

Erin had never been treated like this in all of her sheltered life, and she opened her mouth to tell him so. But one look at Jason's firm jaw convinced her to follow instructions. As she started toward the dressing table, she couldn't resist one barbed shot.

"There are some men who like me the way I am," she told him, stung into angry indiscretion.

He grabbed her arm savagely and pulled her around to face him. "Is that who you were waiting for tonight?"

"What are you talking about?" She was honestly puzzled.

"Don't play the innocent maiden with me!" Jason's face was carved out of granite. "Were you waiting for Brad? Is that why you were dressed like that when I came in?" His lip curled. "Or undressed, I should say."

Erin flinched and turned even paler. Her lips quivered as she whispered, "You can't believe that."

His eyes searched her face and there was some powerful emotion flickering in their depths. "I don't know what to believe anymore. Could I really be so wrong about you?" He held her face between his palms and looked deep into her sapphire eyes. "You're so heartbreakingly beautiful," he murmured in a husky voice, bending his head toward her.

A shiver ran through Erin and for a moment she felt actually ill. He believed all those terrible things about her and Brad and yet he still wanted to make love to her! Or maybe that enhanced her desirability. Had he decided she was an experienced woman who would give him great pleasure in bed? Well, he would never find out. It was at that precise moment that Erin realized that no matter what he did to her, she couldn't go through with the bargain.

Her legs were trembling and her mouth was dry, but she forced the words out. "Let me go home, Jason. I'm sorry, but this whole trip was a mistake. I thought I could go through with it, but I can't."

His passion slowly receded as he looked at the miserable girl confronting him. Lighting a cigarette, he inhaled deeply. "Aren't you forgetting something?" he asked ironically.

The ten thousand dollars, of course. He still had that to hold over her head. How could she possibly raise it? There *had* to be another solution. Squaring her shoulders, she said, "I'll pay off the money some other way. Maybe . . . maybe I can borrow it," she added desperately, although she couldn't imagine where.

His face hardened. "Brad is a very rich man, but I think you'll find his interest rates are the same as mine."

The enormity of his suspicions took her breath away. "You're detestable!" she cried. "I wasn't thinking of Brad. I don't want anything to do with him—or you, either. I just want to go home."

His face was cruel and there was no longer any desire in it, just grim determination. Erin's head drooped with the realization that she was completely at his mercy and there was nothing she could do about it. She didn't even have enough money for her fare home.

Putting his finger under her chin, he forced her to look at him. "Right now, we're going to a party and you're going to pretend you enjoy being with me."

Mercifully, the ride to the Detweiler house was short, because they drove it in complete silence. Jason seemed preoccupied with his thoughts and

Erin languished in the farthest corner of the front seat, a small bundle of misery.

When they reached the house, he helped her out in a perfunctory manner and escorted her inside. As usual, there was a large crowd, and many of the same people present had been at Jason's the night before. Erin found herself being greeted as part of the group, and, to her surprise, Jason stayed by her side as though he were truly her escort. Or was he afraid she might somehow manage to escape before he was through tormenting her, Erin wondered bitterly?

Bibi materialized out of the crowd and looked at Erin in surprise. "You changed your mind! That's great, but how did you get here?"

"I went back and picked her up," Jason said without further explanation.

Bibi looked at them speculatively, but all she said was, "I see."

Tommy joined them then and showed surprise also. "Well, look who came to the party. Glad to see you, Erin. How did Jason get you to change your mind?"

Before she could answer, Jason smiled mockingly at her and said, "I have hidden powers of persuasion, don't I, my love?"

He slipped his arm around her waist and pulled her to him. For a moment her head rested against his hard shoulder before she strained against his encircling arm. But it was like a steel band and she was forced to let him hold her, terribly conscious of the warmth of his body next to hers.

"Jason, I've been looking all over for you. Where on earth have you been?" Veronica's petulant voice demanded his immediate attention.

For the first time, Jason showed irritation with his beautiful blond houseguest. Barely containing his annoyance, he said, "Veronica, surely you must have something better to do than keep tabs on me all evening."

Her face flushed an ugly red and she snapped, "How dare you talk to me like that."

"I seem to be the only one who can, my dear," he drawled insolently.

"You think I'll take anything from you, don't you?" Her voice had risen shrilly and people were turning around to look.

"Lower your voice, Veronica." Jason's tone was deadly.

"You can't tell me what to do," she shot back furiously, seemingly intent on making a scene.

Erin was horrified and shrank back into the crowd. There was no telling what Veronica might say. She was working herself into a tantrum, and Erin didn't want to be her next target. Making her way to the farthest side of the room seemed to be the safest idea.

Bibi found her there and remarked, "Our Veronica is in rare form tonight, isn't she? Don't worry about it, though; nobody pays any attention. This time Jason doesn't seem in the mood to calm her down, but that's all to the good. Either she'll toe the mark tomorrow or else. Either way we win."

"Does she do this often?" Erin asked.

"Often enough."

"But I don't understand. Why do people put up with her?"

Bibi shrugged. "I guess it has something to do with the fact that most of us have known each other all our lives. Or maybe we just feel sorry for her."

"Sorry for her!" Erin cried, unable to credit this explanation. "How could you? She has everything!"

Bibi looked at her pityingly. "When will you accept the fact, Erin, that you have more."

The rest of the evening passed in an uneasy blur for Erin. She spent most of it staying out of Jason's path. At times, she saw him searching for her, but the frown on his face convinced her to move in the opposite direction. Avoiding Veronica was automatic. Erin didn't feel up to a battle of wits with either of them, and the effort to be on her guard was exhausting.

At some point, most of the party moved to another house where a buffet supper was laid out. Erin dutifully accompanied Bibi and Tommy. She couldn't eat a morsel, but at least she was with her good friends and she stuck unobtrusively close to them.

Finally, Bibi started to yawn and said, "I've about had it. How about you, Erin?"

"Oh, yes!" Erin's answer was so heartfelt that Bibi grinned. "Just let me tell Jason I'm going and I'll be right back."

She couldn't make the mistake again of merely disappearing. Jason had made it abundantly clear that he had paid for her time and was entitled to an accounting. Spotting him across the room, Erin approached him diffidently.

"Bibi and Tommy are going home now. Do you mind if I go with them?"

He looked searchingly over the crowd. When he glimpsed them waiting in the doorway, his face relaxed. "If you like," he said indifferently.

It obviously made no difference to him whether she went or stayed, and Erin felt like an idiot for having disturbed him. "Well . . . good night," she said uncertainly.

"Good night." His enigmatic eyes held hers for a long moment. "Perhaps I'll see you later."

Erin was silent in the car going home, but nobody noticed. Bibi chattered on about the party and

Tommy concentrated on his driving, punctuating it with massive yawns. When they parted in the hall, Erin was keyed up like a finely tuned instrument.

What did Jason's last words to her mean? Were they a warning that he didn't intend to let her out of her promise in spite of her plea that she couldn't go through with it? If that were the case, there would be nothing she could do. Erin knew from bitter experience that he was capable of forcing her to submit to his superior male strength. Was tonight the night? And, if so, would he take her more gently than that terrible last time?

Erin undressed and slipped beneath the covers, her whole body taut with uncertainty. She stared at the ceiling, willing herself to relax, but Jason was a tangible presence in her bed. She could almost feel his hard body covering hers, and, with a shiver, she covered her breasts with her arms.

The minutes ticked by unnoticed, and Erin didn't know how much later it was that she heard muted voices in the hall. Jason and Veronica had returned.

She waited, unbearably tense in the darkness, but her bedroom door remained closed. After a while the house grew silent. A long time later, Erin fell asleep.

Chapter Seven

Breakfast at Jason's house was an informal affair that would have driven most servants to give notice, but Rosa and Manolo didn't seem to mind. Everyone ate whenever he felt like it, and, unless otherwise specified, the food was laid out English style on a long marble buffet in the dining room. There were pitchers of iced fruit juices and covered silver chafing dishes that kept the eggs and ham and sausages piping hot. A silver service at one end held coffee and tea, and there were baskets of blueberry muffins and small coffee cakes.

When Erin came in to breakfast the next morning, she found everyone but Veronica already assembled. Helping herself to a plate, she joined them at the long, polished dining room table.

"Did you sleep well, Erin?" Jason asked.

She looked at him warily. Surely it was just a polite question from a solicitous host, but why did she detect a sardonic gleam in his eye? Or was there? She had got into the habit of examining his smallest utterance, which was fruitless. She still couldn't figure him out.

"I was telling them about our trip yesterday, Erin, and even these dyed-in-the-wool sophisticates had to admit it sounded like fun," Bibi said. "How about some more sightseeing today? There are loads of interesting places on the island."

Erin's face lit up. "I'd love it!" She looked uncertainly at Jason. "Would you mind?"

"Not at all. As a matter of fact, Tommy and I will join you."

"Speak for yourself, buddy," Tommy warned.

"All right, then I'll take the girls," Jason said.

He was all affability this morning. Although Erin didn't care to examine the reasons for it, she was grateful that he was in a good mood.

"Don't be such a party pooper, Tommy," his wife advised. "It won't hurt you to come along. I thought we'd go to Rose Hall Great House today. How does that sound?"

"What is it?" Erin asked curiously.

"Rose Hall is one of the most famous of the old plantations that flourished in the seventeen hundreds. There are all kinds of legends about it, mainly because of Annie Palmer, a sadistic beauty who ran the place with an iron hand. She was noted for her cruelty."

"Was she English?" Erin asked.

"Partly. She was born in Haiti of an English mother and an Irish father, and the story goes that she learned black magic from the local witch doctors. The natives called her the White Witch of Rose Hall, and they truly believed she had supernatural powers."

"She also had three husbands who all came to a bad end," Jason added. "She claimed one was an alcoholic, one went mad and the third died of natural causes, but the natives gave a different version. They called it poison, stabbing, and strangulation," he said dryly.

"Her slaves didn't have it much easier," Tommy

chimed in. "She used to ride around the property at night in men's clothes with a huge whip that she used on anyone she found roaming about. I think she rode a black stallion. That's fitting, isn't it?"

"You've just given me a great idea," Bibi exclaimed. "Rose Hall covers thousands of acres. Why don't we rent some horses and tour the estate on horseback?"

Tommy was doubtful. "I'm not sure you're allowed. I know you can ride through Good Hope Estate at Falmouth, but I don't know about Rose Hall."

"Jason can arrange it," Bibi assured him. "He has influence everywhere."

Jason smiled. "I'm flattered by your confidence in me." Turning to Erin, he asked, "Do you ride?"

"Not very well," she admitted, "but I'm sure I could manage to stay on, as long as you don't mind how I look doing it. I was a regular customer at the pony track when I was little, if that helps any."

"You'll be fine. We'll get you a gentle horse," Bibi assured her. "Then it's all settled."

"What's all settled?" Veronica had entered the dining room and was looking at them questioningly.

"We were just planning an outing to Rose Hall today and a horseback ride around the grounds."

"Are you still on that sightseeing kick?" Veronica asked disgustedly.

Bibi looked at her with narrowed eyes. "No one's forcing you to go."

"Of course I'm not going," Veronica said. "Dwayne and Karen's yacht is due back this morning and a group of us are going to have lunch on board. Isn't it a divine day for it, darling?" she asked Jason, apparently completely over her pique of the night before.

Erin looked at Jason apprehensively. He had

evidently forgotten his date with Veronica. Did that mean the rest of them would have to give up their plans also?

But she needn't have worried. Jason was saying, "I'm sorry, but the four of us are going to Rose Hall. You can go to lunch with the others if you'd rather."

"I don't want to go with them. I want to be with you." Veronica's lower lip was jutting out like a thwarted child's.

"Then come to Rose Hall," he told her reasonably.

"Why can't we go to lunch?"

Jason's patience, never his long suit, was wearing dangerously thin. "Make up your mind, Veronica. We'll meet out front in half an hour. And if you're coming, wear jeans," he called over his shoulder.

When Erin stepped out the front door right on time, she found Jason standing beside the most remarkable car she had ever seen. It looked as though it had been driven right out of the pages of an F. Scott Fitzgerald novel. Low and racy, it had a long squared off hood decorated with gleaming curved pipes on either side. The convertible canvas roof was fastened to the windshield with a long row of shiny round snaps and the interior was upholstered in the finest glove leather.

"I have no idea what it is, but that's the most beautiful car I've ever seen," Erin gasped, touching the dark green paint gently.

"Isn't she a beauty?" Jason agreed. "It's called an Excalibur. Would you like to drive it?"

Erin's eyes shone. "Could I really?"

"Of course." He smiled down at her. "Would you like the top up or down?"

"Oh, down, please. I love convertibles."

As Jason started to unfasten the top, Bibi and Veronica joined them. Erin had hoped that Veronica would opt for lunch over sightseeing, which she obviously loathed, but she was evidently determined to put up with anything to be with Jason. It didn't augur well for their outing. She was bound to make someone suffer for her disappointment and wouldn't mind if she spoiled the day for everyone.

As though to prove the point, she called sharply to Jason, "Are you putting the top up?"

He glanced up briefly. "No, I'm putting it down."

"Well, put it back up. You know I can't stand the wind making a mess of my hair."

Tommy was backing a small yellow luxury coupe out of the garage. Jason said, "You can ride with Tommy and Bibi."

"I don't want to go with them. I want to be with you. Why do you think I'm coming on this stupid tour, anyway?"

Jason eyed her impassively. "You can go with them or you can stay home. Erin and I are driving the Excalibur—with the top down," he added firmly.

Veronica's thin lips curled back, exposing clenched teeth. "What makes you think I'm going to put up with those arrangements? You've humiliated me for the last time, Jason Dimitriou! I don't have to take that kind of treatment from you or any man! I'm leaving, do you hear me? When you get back, I won't be here," she shouted, and stamped furiously into the house.

Erin stood by in an agony of embarrassment, but Jason was completely unruffled. "Get behind the wheel and I'll adjust the seat for you," he said, as though nothing had happened.

Erin's heart swelled with happiness. It didn't seem possible, but he didn't care if Veronica left! Slipping obediently into the front seat, she looked at the top of his head as he bent over, appalled at herself because she had an almost uncontrollable urge to run her fingers through his thick black hair. As he straightened up, he caught her watching him and their eyes met. She dropped hers in confusion, afraid she had given herself away and he would guess why she was suddenly having trouble breathing.

His hand reached out and gently caressed the soft skin of her neck under the tumbling mane of shining hair. "Erin . . ."

"Okay, troops, let's get going," Tommy's voice called.

As the little yellow car roared past them down the driveway, Jason walked around and got in the passenger seat. Erin's breathing was still uneven, but Jason seemed unaffected by the small moment of intimacy. He gave her last-minute instructions.

"Take it easy until you get the feel of her. This little devil can go like the wind. Before you know it, you're doing ninety."

Erin promised to be careful, but when they got out on the highway and she felt the powerful car surge under her, she unconsciously stepped down on the gas pedal. The wind lifted her long hair, whipping it wildly around her excited face. Jason moved close to her, gathering the silken strands in one hand so her view was unimpeded. He studied her tilted nose and the contours of her soft mouth, but for once Erin wasn't conscious of his nearness.

"Oh, Jason, this is so wonderful. I'll bet this is what flying feels like!"

He kissed her hair so lightly that she was unaware of the caress. "I know, but you'd better slow down, little one."

Looking at the speedometer, Erin was aghast and eased up on the accelerator. "You were right. I had no idea we were going so fast."

When they reached the stables, Tommy took charge of selecting horses. The mare he chose for

Erin was named Sunshine and guaranteed to be docile. Looking at its eyes as it turned its head to look at her, Erin had some misgivings, but not for the world would she have admitted it.

The ride to Rose Hall was through gently wooded slopes, and Erin gradually overcame her nervousness. When Bibi and Tommy cantered on ahead, she was all for joining their pace, but Jason restrained her.

"I want you to get the feel of it first. We have all day."

"But I'm holding you back," she protested. "This can't be any fun for you."

He smiled at her. "Don't bet on it."

A wave of delight swept over Erin. Maybe this was only a truce, but he was telling her that he was enjoying being with her. No matter what came after, she had a feeling this was going to be a golden day in her memories.

Nothing they had told her prepared Erin for her first look at Rose Hall. The serene three-story mansion nestled among towering trees and belied its bloody history. Wide balconies invited sunning, and the huge mahogany doors with high ornamented arches looked hospitable.

Inside, the polished floors had been restored to their former magnificence and everything spoke of money and ease, but there were subtle reminders of the former owner's cruelty. How many slaves had it taken to fashion those hand-hewn stone steps that led to the music salon and countless guest rooms? And in Annie's great bedroom, where she finally met a violent end at the hands of grossly abused servants, were there actually duppies, or ghosts, as some Jamaicans still claimed? Erin shivered. Although she enjoyed the tour, she was nevertheless glad to get out into the warm fresh air.

The large pond, at least, held no memories of evil. The regal swans floating on its glassy surface appeared almost unreal in their perfection. The small island in the middle, filled with brilliantly flowering shrubs, was an added delight.

After giving Erin time to look her fill, Bibi called, "Okay, everybody, time to get on our horses—literally," and they all mounted up.

Only a short distance from the house, or so it seemed, they were back in the seventeen hundreds. Huge tree ferns, still standing after centuries, waved their feathered fans at broad-leafed banana trees that whispered softly back. Their dense green formed a backdrop for flaming poincianas, African tulip trees and pink oleanders, while citrus of every kind contributed their perfume. Civilization with its horns and radios was far away, and harmonious sounds took their rightful place in this sylvan wonderland. Bird songs filled the air and secretive rustlings stirred the underbrush, hinting at a hidden world.

Bibi and Tommy had gone crashing on ahead, and this time Erin was happy to let them go. She wanted time to savor the peace and quiet of this enchanted spot.

Looking at her rapt expression, Jason asked gently, "Are you happy, Erin?"

"Oh, yes, it's the most beautiful place I've ever seen. Thank you for bringing me."

He smiled down at her excited face, but she wasn't aware of it. Looking past his shoulder, she cried, "Look! Aren't those orchids over there?"

Without turning, he said, "I wouldn't be surprised. There are two hundred varieties growing wild in Jamaica."

Impulsively slipping off her horse, Erin ran over to inspect the exotic pale green blossoms, which on closer inspection had centers of brilliant scarlet. Jason joined her, but when he reached toward them, she caught his hand.

"No, no, don't pick them. We must leave everything exactly as it is."

He ruffled her hair fondly. "You're a funny woman. They wouldn't mind if you took one."

She shook her head. "I just like to look at them. There's something so exciting about finding them in the wild."

He slipped his arm around her shoulders, and it felt completely natural. "Let's walk for a while and maybe we'll find some more."

With the horses trailing lazily after them, they strolled through the woods. To her delight, Erin found several other varieties. She crooned over little purple orchids with delicate pansy faces and knelt down to inspect yellow ones with bright orange splashes while Jason followed indulgently.

But finally, with obvious reluctance, he said, "I think we'd better catch up with Bibi and Tommy."

Erin had almost forgotten about them, but she agreed immediately. "Of course. They must be miles ahead of us."

They got back on their horses and this time speeded up the pace. Jason went ahead to lead the way and Erin followed on the fat mare, who was indignant at being expected to do more than a fast walk.

It happened as they passed an especially dense part of the trail. Jason's horse scared up a small animal that became so startled it jumped back on the path instead of into the dense underbrush on either side. Erin's mare reared in alarm, and before she even knew what happened, a low overhanging branch swept her to the ground with a sickening thud. Fortunately, she landed in a bed of soft leaves, but the fall took her breath away and she couldn't even cry out.

Jason was off his horse in a flash and he gathered her in his arms. "Erin, are you all right?" His voice was taut with apprehension.

She opened her eyes and tried to speak, to reassure him, but the words wouldn't come. In her dazed state, she thought she saw terror on his face, but that couldn't be. Jason wasn't afraid of anything.

"Darling, tell me where it hurts," he begged, pasty white under his tan.

Finally, her breath returned enough to say, "I'm all right, just shaken up a bit. Sunshine reared and that branch knocked me off."

He gathered her to him in a smothering embrace and she could feel his heart beating wildly. "Thank God," he breathed. "Oh, thank God!"

With her nose mashed against his chest, she said with difficulty, "I'm sorry I was so clumsy, but something ran across the path and I didn't expect it."

He released her long enough to look at her searchingly. There was a smudge on her cheekbone and he probed it with gentle fingers. "Does that hurt?" When she shook her head, his feather touch explored every part of her face and then the back of her head, anxiously looking for bruises. There was a very small lump at the base of her hairline, and she winced when he touched it.

"Does that hurt?"

"Just a little bit," she admitted. He leaned over and kissed it, and she laughed, peering up through her tangled mane. "You must have had a mother like mine. She always believed you could kiss away the bumps."

But he didn't laugh with her. His face was somber as he said, "If anything had happened to you . . ."

Erin looked up at him in wonderment. She had

never seen him like this, so tender and caring. He cradled her and his hand stroked her cheek. It seemed like an awful lot of concern for such a little accident, but she snuggled happily in his arms until honesty prompted her to say, "It wasn't anything serious, Jason."

He remained unconvinced, and his voice was ragged as he said, "If you'd hit your head on a rock . . ." He tightened his hold convulsively. "My little doll, what would I have done?"

Erin's heartbeat matched his. Did that mean he really cared? Not the way you would naturally care about anyone who had had an accident, but *really* cared? He had caused her so much pain and torment. Was this just another passing mood?

His fingers were gently combing bits of leaves from her hair, carefully avoiding the sore spot. Erin relaxed in his arms. Life could hold very few sweeter moments, but, like all good things, it couldn't last forever. A crashing in the distance heralded the arrival of Tommy and Bibi, coming back to see where they were.

"Lie down and rest for a minute," Jason told her, spreading his handkerchief under her head.

When the Exeters arrived and saw Erin stretched out on the ground, immediate concern gripped them.

"What happened?" Bibi cried, jumping down from her horse.

"Erin had a little accident, but I think she's all right," Jason told them, explaining the circumstances.

"Poor baby," Bibi exclaimed, rushing over to examine Erin, who felt like a fool.

"I'm fine, really. Jason's making much too much out of it. I just had the wind knocked out of me."

"We'd better get her to a doctor," Tommy said.

"No! I don't need a doctor. There's nothing wrong with me," Erin assured them.

Bibi's expression was anxious. "Are you sure?"

"Of course." Erin struggled to sit up. "I'm getting back on that dumb horse and we're continuing our ride. How can I convince you?"

"I think you just did," Bibi said, smiling at her.

She got back on the mare, but the others insisted on returning to the stables. By then it was late afternoon, so Erin didn't feel too guilty about it. Jason fretted over her all the way home.

When they got to the house, he wanted to carry her inside and was dissuaded with great difficulty.

"Jason, do stop fussing over me. It's not like I broke anything." But when she reached back for her purse, a twinge of pain shot through her shoulder and she winced.

"What's wrong?" He scooped her up in his arms in spite of her protests and examined her worriedly.

"It's nothing, really. I must have twisted my arm slightly. It just hurt a little when I reached in back of me, but it isn't anything serious."

"I'll be the judge of that," he said grimly, carrying her to her room. "I'm going to put you to bed."

"Jason, no! There's that fancy party at the club tonight, and I don't want to miss it."

"Not on your life!" he told her firmly.

The color had returned to his face, and his autocratic manner along with it, Erin thought wryly. "Please, Jason, it's only five o'clock," she pleaded. "If I promise to rest for a while, can't I please go tonight?"

At first he was adamant, but she had her heart set on going, which was quite funny. Ordinarily, she would have welcomed any excuse to get out of one of their endless parties, but tonight was different. If Veronica really meant what she said about leaving,

Erin would have Jason all to herself. The idea was so intoxicating that she begged quite shamelessly. With her smudged face and pleading manner, she looked adorable. Jason's eyes softened.

"Well . . . if you're sure you're up to it," he gave in reluctantly.

"Oh, I am! Honestly, I am. I'll take a hot bath and soak out all the kinks. I'll be as good as new."

Her face was tilted eagerly up to his and he put his hands on her shoulders. Something flickered deep in his eyes, and Erin's senses quickened as she wondered if he was going to take her in his arms. But instead, he turned her around and she heard the soft purr of her zipper being unzipped. Then, before she could stop him, he unhooked her bra.

Clutching her blouse to her, Erin gasped, "What are you doing?"

She started to turn around to face him, but he slid his arms around her waist, pulling her against him and kissing the back of her neck. "You said it hurt to reach around. How did you expect to get out of your clothes?"

Erin's rigid body relaxed and she felt foolish. "I don't know," she mumbled.

He kissed the soft skin behind her ear and sudden waves of feeling swept over her. "Well, now you know."

His warm mouth was traveling down her back, pausing sensuously at each bump of her spine, and her pulses started to throb like a tom-tom. She leaned weakly against him, all will to resist long gone, and he held her for a delicious moment.

Erin was floating on a pink cloud of happiness. It came as a rude shock when he gave her a firm pat on the bottom and ordered, "Now go get in a hot tub."

When she turned around, he was going out the door.

Chapter Eight

The party at the yacht club that Erin was so determined to attend was a costume party. The theme was "Caribbean Night," and all the guests were supposed to dress in their version of native attire. This left a wide latitude, but at least the men were guaranteed comfort for one night, freed of their usual coats and ties.

After Erin had convinced Bibi that she was feeling fine, the two women discussed their costumes.

"I have a couple of sarongs that I think would be just perfect," Bibi said. "They might be more South Seas than Caribbean, but who's to know?" She rummaged in her drawer and came up with two brightly colored lengths of cloth. "This one will be darling on you, Erin."

It was brilliantly patterned in large flowers of purple and fuchsia on a white background. Erin accepted it gratefully.

"It's beautiful, Bibi. How can I thank you? You're always doing nice things for me."

Looking at her friend's radiant face, Bibi commented, "It looks like you and Jason patched things up. Didn't I tell you everything would be okay as soon as we got rid of Veronica and Brad?"

The words gave Erin pause. In spite of the truce, Jason's bitter suspicions about her and Brad still hung over her like a cloud. He had never said he believed her. And Veronica was gone, but was she really forgotten? However, she refused to dwell on anything unpleasant tonight. Surely nothing could go wrong on this charmed day, and tomorrow was far away. She was completely carefree as she went to her room to dress.

After securing the knot on her sarong, Erin wasn't quite as serene. The exotic garment was a great deal more revealing than she had bargained for. Her creamy shoulders rose bare above the strapless top as she had expected, but the side-slit skirt disclosed an alarming amount of naked thigh and was extremely short to boot. Erin's legs were long and lovely, but she was dubious about displaying so much of them. Which was silly, really. A bikini revealed a whole lot more. What was there about appearing half naked at night that was so much more seductive?

A knock sounded at the door and Bibi entered, carrying a square white florist's box. "Jason sent us orchids. Isn't he a lamb?"

Opening hers, Erin found a spray of small purple blossoms. She felt as ecstatic as a schoolgirl with her first corsage.

Looking over her shoulder, Bibi cried, "Those will be absolutely perfect in your hair. Sit down, Erin, and let me fix them for you."

Positioning her in front of the mirror, Bibi deftly lifted the hair at Erin's temples, securing the shiny strands with a wreath of orchids like a halo across the top of her head. The rest of her hair hung down like a thick auburn cloud and curved softly around her slender shoulders.

Surveying her handiwork, Bibi gave a satisfied nod. "You look smashing. Wait till they get a load of you at the club tonight. You'll knock them dead."

Erin gazed in the mirror and her eyes were wistful. There was only one person whose attention she wanted. Would Jason think she looked smashing? Inspecting her image critically, she automatically tried to pull up the sarong where her young breasts swelled gently over the top, but Bibi stopped her.

"Leave it alone, it's perfect just the way it is. You look sexy as all get out."

Erin looked at her doubtfully. She didn't want to look sexy; she wanted Jason's love, not his passion. And yet . . . deep down in the recesses of her mind, Erin knew that she wanted this man any way he would have her.

Blushing at the thought, she picked up her purse to cover her confusion and said to Bibi, "I'm ready if you are."

When they joined the men, Tommy gave a low whistle, including both of them in his admiration. But it was the look on Jason's face that made a small pulse start to beat at the base of Erin's graceful throat. His eyes were gray coals of fire, and her long lashes shyly drooped before the blaze.

Taking her small rounded chin in his palm, he forced her to look at him. "That color is very becoming on you," he smiled.

Erin was having difficulty with her breathing, but she managed to say, "Thank you for the orchids. They're lovely."

"You seemed to like them so much today. It was the least I could do."

"Oh, but I wasn't asking for anything," Erin protested, aghast that he should think she had been hinting.

He took both of her hands in his warm grasp. "You never do. That's the wonder of you."

"How's the old noggin, Erin?" Tommy asked.

"I'm fine," she assured him. "Not even a head-ache. I must have a very hard head."

"Great! Then if everybody's ready, we can get going."

Festivities were in full swing by the time they got to the yacht club, which was gaily decorated for the occasion. Balloons and larger-than-life paper flowers decorated the room, and all the tables were lit by the soft glow of candles surrounded by fragrant fresh floral arrangements.

Everyone was dressed in costume and some of the men rivaled the women in splendor, with brightly patterned shirts that were tied at the waist instead of buttoned. There were also a few men in pirate costumes scattered about the room.

Their progress was impeded while Jason and the Exeters greeted their many friends, but eventually they were shown to their table. After they had ordered a drink, Jason asked Erin to dance and she preceded him happily onto the floor.

He took her in his arms and she almost shivered with delight as her soft body molded to his hard, demanding one. His tanned chest was bare through the open shirt and she nestled her cheek against the curly black hair that showed through. For this moment, at least, he was all hers, and Erin closed her eyes and let herself dream the impossible. This man, holding her so lovingly was her husband. When they went home a little later, he would make exquisite, tender love to her, and his hands and body would bring blessed relief from the longing she felt whenever he was near.

"You're very quiet, Erin." His low voice called her back to reality. "What are you thinking about?"

He was studying her face intently and she blushed under those penetrating gray eyes, afraid they might guess her fantasy. She couldn't bear the cool amusement her silly dream would afford him.

"I . . . nothing. I was just thinking what a wonderful party this is," she said in answer to his question.

"And as usual, you're the prettiest girl here," he said, bending down to kiss the hollow of her throat.

"Jason!" Erin was scandalized. "What are people going to think?"

He threw back his head and laughed. "These people? If they happened to notice, it would be just like a handshake to them, you little innocent."

The idea depressed Erin and reminded her of the big difference in their backgrounds. "I guess I must seem very unsophisticated to you," she said uncertainly.

He held her so close she could hear the steady beat of his heart. "Not unsophisticated, my darling. Just young and very vulnerable."

Erin had never considered the difference in their ages. Was that another obstacle? "I'm not that young," she protested. "I'll be twenty any day now."

He inspected her flawless skin minutely, touching the corner of her eye with a gentle forefinger. "Yes, I do believe I see the start of a wrinkle."

"Jason, be serious. You're treating me like a child and I'm not."

"How would you like me to treat you?" he asked.

She knew he was only teasing her, but the low caressing tone of his voice was upsetting, causing a thrill to pass through her whole body. A delicate pink flushed her cheeks and her soft mouth parted slightly as she looked up at him through shaded lashes, not knowing quite how to reply.

"My dear Erin, if you're trying to convince me that you're a woman, you've just succeeded," he said dryly. "But I wouldn't suggest you practice that seductive look on any of the other men here tonight. They may not have my willpower."

"I wasn't doing anything," she protested.

"Then you're in more danger than I thought, my naive little beauty. Some of these pirates would carry you off in a minute. I can see where I'll have to stay by your side all evening."

Nothing could have made Erin happier, and she wriggled blissfully in his arms. Unfortunately, her euphoria lasted only until they returned to the table.

They had been joined by the group from Dwayne and Karen's yacht, and among the newcomers was Brad Honeywell. He jumped up and gave them a big greeting, shaking Jason's hand and giving Erin a light kiss on the cheek. She recoiled in disgust. How could he act as though nothing had happened between them? Surely he knew how she felt about him! But already the damage was done. Jason's face wore that closed, secret look she had come to dread. He was the soul of courtesy, though, asking Brad about his trip.

"The fishing was great, Jase," Brad answered. "You would have loved it. And we stopped off and spent some time with the Courtneys in St. Croix."

"Where to now?" Jason asked.

"Well, that's the thing." Brad seemed slightly embarrassed. "I was wondering if I could have my old room back?"

"Did you wear out your welcome with Dwayne or with Karen?" On the surface, Jason's words were just the cheerful banter between friends, but his mouth was grim.

"Nothing like that." Brad was aggrieved. "It's just that Karen has some relatives flying in and there isn't room. So, how about it?"

Jason shrugged. "Sure, why not? We're leaving tomorrow, anyway." Erin drew in her breath sharply and he turned to her. "I was going to tell you later. I got a long distance call when we returned this afternoon and it's something that just won't wait. I'm sorry."

Erin looked up at this tall, autocratic man who had become the center of her universe in such a short time and willed herself not to cry. It had to end some time, she had always known that. It was just that it was so unexpected. And it came at the wrong time. Just when she had begun to hope that maybe . . .

Jason was watching her with grave eyes, waiting for her reaction. Mustering all of her composure, Erin said cooly, "Of course, I understand."

He quirked a sardonic eyebrow at her. "And I can tell you're devastated by the news."

That wasn't fair! What did he expect her to do, beg him to stay? And why would he want to? Until today, the trip had been a disaster. He had acted as though he couldn't stand the sight of her. Then this afternoon, by some miracle—maybe because she had fallen off the horse and he felt somehow responsible—he had been charming to her. Which made everything even worse. She wished today had never happened. After they left the island, it was unlikely that she would ever see him again. It would have been easier never knowing his tenderness, never feeling the wild beat of his heart against hers or the frantic clutch of his arms holding her as if he would never let go.

He was standing over her, waiting for some comment on his cynical remark. Striving for an indifferent tone, Erin said, "This trip was your idea. I have nothing to say about it."

His eyes narrowed to gray chips of ice and the skin

tightened over his high cheekbones as he said, "I'm sorry it's been such an ordeal, but I remember at least once when you were enjoying yourself very much."

She knew he was referring to that horrible night on the beach with Brad, and she was too hurt and miserable to deny it further. Stung into impulsive speech, she said, "I know how that must have distressed you. The idea was for you to enjoy yourself not me, wasn't it?"

His lip curled with distaste and he looked at her contemptuously. "So you haven't forgotten why you're here? I was beginning to wonder." He looked her up and down as if she were a piece of marked-down merchandise. "But now I'm not really sure I want you."

Erin's face paled and an actual pain stabbed through her breast. Why had she said such a foolish, crazy thing? Now he would never believe in her innocence. Oh, what difference did it make? It was all so hopeless, anyway!

They were standing very close together, a small oasis in the swirling gaiety around them. Brad had moved away quickly after he had got Jason's permission to return, probably afraid his host might change his mind. And nobody noticed the tense couple amid all the noise and laughter because, in spite of the tension crackling between them, they had instinctively kept their voices low.

Her eyes fell before the cruel appraisal in his, and, grabbing her purse, she said, "If you'll excuse me, I'm going to the powder room."

Fortunately, there was no one she knew there. Erin gripped the edge of the dressing table, taking deep breaths to steady herself. She looked in the mirror, not really seeing the pale, distraught woman

who stared back. When a measure of calm returned
and she realized it was her own image, Erin was
aghast. She rummaged about for a lipstick, but even
as her shaking fingers closed over it, she knew that
no amount of makeup could cover the scars Jason's
words had inflicted.

How could she go back out there and face his cold
contempt? For a wild moment, Erin considered
running away. Even as the idea surfaced, she knew it
was impossible. Run where? There was no escape,
and he would hate her even more for being a
coward. No, she would have to go back and take her
punishment. It was just one more thing that had to
be endured.

Squaring her shoulders gallantly, she pushed open
the door. But before she had gone more than a few
steps, she bumped into Brad.

"I've been waiting for you, Erin. I want to talk to
you."

She looked at him with deep distaste. "We have
nothing to say to each other."

He tried to take her hands and she snatched them
away angrily. "I want to apologize," he pleaded.

"There isn't anything you can say that would make
me forgive you! The only decent thing you did was
go away, and you had to spoil even that by coming
back. Why couldn't you have waited until tomorrow?"

His face was set in lines of deep contrition. "I
know how you feel. If it's any consolation to you, I
hate myself as much as you do. My only excuse is
that you were so irresistible in the moonlight." His
eyes drank in her full mouth, compressed now in
anger, and the fringed deep blue eyes, alive in the
delicate oval of her face. For a moment, a predatory
male look came over him, but he quickly extin-

guished it. "And I was blind drunk," he added penitently.

"And you think that's an excuse?" she asked scornfully.

"Not an excuse; just an abject plea for forgiveness." His handsome weak face was looking at her pleadingly. She couldn't imagine why, but for a fleeting moment he reminded her of Bob.

"What difference does it make if I forgive you or not?" she asked wearily. Everything was spoiled now, anyway.

"It makes a lot of difference to me." They were approaching the table and he stopped her. "I care about your opinion. I swear to you I've never before done anything like that in my life. Won't you believe me?"

Erin sighed. His explanation sounded convincing enough, and she couldn't really go on hating Brad. She didn't care that much about him. "All right, I believe you."

Grasping her shoulders lightly, he said, "And you forgive me?"

She smiled wanly into his anxious face. "Yes, I forgive you."

Turning toward the table, she saw Jason's hard stare and her heart sank. He would probably choose to misinterpret this the way he did all of her encounters with Brad. As though to prove it, he turned deliberately to the woman on his right, leaving Brad to help Erin into her chair.

The music started and Brad asked her to dance, but she refused so firmly that he very wisely knew not to press her. After he left, she stared down at the tablecloth, drawing intricate designs with her fingernail. Jason was so close she could feel the warmth of his body. His muscular forearm was only inches away from her hand, but he might as well have been on the moon. He ignored her completely, and Erin felt small and lost and lonely.

"Would one of the two prettiest women here care to dance?" a voice asked in her ear.

She looked up and found Tommy smiling at her. Rising gratefully, she accepted his invitation. It was a relief to get away from the table, and Tommy was the only man here with whom she felt comfortable.

"You look a little done in," he said, surveying her critically. "Is that bump on the head acting up?"

"No, I'm fine," she told him, managing a fleeting smile. "I guess I'm just a little bit tired. It's been an eventful day."

"Why don't you have Jason take you home?" His pleasant face showed concern.

"Oh, no! I don't want to spoil the party. He's having such a good time." A little white lie could be forgiven and perhaps it wasn't a lie. Glancing over at the table, she saw him listening attentively to the woman at his side. It was as though Erin didn't exist and the ugly words between them had never been spoken. How did he turn off his emotions so easily? But the answer to that was simple. He just didn't care. His only feeling toward her was revulsion.

"Tell you what," Tommy was saying. "I'll run you home myself. A brief respite from one of these shindigs my wife is so addicted to can only come as a blessing."

"Thank you, but I want to stay, truly I do," she told him. It was another fib, but she was afraid to invite Jason's anger any further. She knew that he expected her to stay by his side and pretend nothing had happened. That was part of her punishment and a sop to his pride.

"Well, if you're sure," Tommy gave in reluctantly.

Jason's cruelty was exquisite for the rest of the endless evening. His manners were impeccable as always, but he paid just enough attention to Erin to satisfy convention. The majority of his time was lavished on the other women at the table.

When one of them remarked that it was too bad they were leaving so soon, Jason said, "Yes, it's especially sad for Erin." He turned a hard smile on her. "She thoroughly enjoyed frolicking on the beach, didn't you, my love?"

Erin made a strangled sound and started to rise, but he pulled her back down, his fingers biting into her soft arm. Oh, how she hated him at that moment! She was like a small animal caught in a cruel trap, and he was enjoying her struggles to get free. She glared at him, and a small sardonic smile played around his mouth as his fingers increased their pressure. He was daring her to protest, and then he would tighten the noose with words that sounded innocent—except to her.

Erin bowed her head. She was no match for this man. At her gesture of submission, the pressure of his hand lessened and he turned away indifferently.

Through a shimmer of misery, Erin finally realized that someone was saying her name. She looked up to see Brad beside her. "Would you change your mind and dance with me?" he asked.

"Oh, yes!" She jumped quickly to her feet before Jason could stop her, but he made no move to do so.

"You don't mind do you, Jason?" Brad asked correctly.

Jason turned a bland look at him. "Of course not. Erin may do whatever she likes."

As Brad's arms closed around her, Erin regretted her impulsive acceptance. His face was flushed, and she could smell a distinct odor of scotch.

Drawing back, she said sharply, "You've been drinking again."

"Only two weak highballs all evening, scout's honor," he said. "You don't think I'd make that mistake again, do you?"

She looked at him doubtfully. It was warm in here with all the people. Even she could feel it. That could account for his flushed face. And he was being a perfect gentleman. He didn't hold her too close and his speech wasn't slurred. Maybe she was being too nervous in the face of his obvious attempt to make amends.

"Have you and Jason had a fight?" he asked unexpectedly.

She was instantly alert. "What makes you think that?"

"Call it intuition." He hesitated and then continued, "I don't know what there is between you two, but if something's gone wrong, I want you to know I'm waiting in the wings. I'm crazy about you, Erin."

"Don't be ridiculous. You barely know me."

"How long does it take?" His eyes were half closed as they fastened on her ripe mouth. "I knew it the minute I saw you."

"Don't look at me like that! You haven't changed and I was an idiot to believe you had." She pulled away from him and would have walked off the floor if he hadn't stopped her, his expression boyishly repentent.

"I'm sorry, Erin. You're just too darn adorable for your own good."

"One more word like that and I'm leaving," she warned.

"No, don't go—I promise."

Against her better judgment, Erin allowed herself to be persuaded. Brad lived up to his word. He was a perfect gentleman and put himself out to be amusing. It was balm to Erin's wounded spirits. She badly needed cheering up, and Brad was adept at that. She was grateful for his efforts and gradually decided not to hold one mistake against him, no matter how horrendous.

It was with reluctance that she returned to the table, and her dread was well founded. Jason was waiting for them tight lipped.

"We have an early plane in the morning. If you don't mind, I'd like to leave." The words were polite but it was a thinly veiled command.

Erin picked up her purse wordlessly as Brad said, "I'm going to stay on for a while. I'll see you later."

The ride home was accomplished in complete silence. Erin opened her mouth once to ask how Bibi and Tommy were getting home, then realized that any number of people would give them a ride. She stole a look at Jason's stern profile, but it was so remote that she felt chilled. Wasn't he ever going to speak to her again? How could she bear the plane ride home?

He stopped in the driveway, leaving the motor running. Leaning across her, he opened the car door and said, "You can go on in. I'm going to put the car away. Be packed and ready by eight o'clock in the morning. I don't expect to have to wait for you." He might have been giving a command to a servant except that his voice would have been less curt.

She slipped out quietly and entered the big house for the last time. Walking forlornly down the hall, Erin felt terribly tired. But she knew that sleep was a blessing not likely to be visited on her tonight. As she stood in the middle of the luxurious bedroom, unanswered questions rained down on her numbed brain. She had made a mess of this whole week, and where did that leave Bob? Would Jason send him to prison now? Even delight in doing so? That way he could destroy both Bradys at once. But even in her bitterness, Erin knew he wasn't that unfair. He might despise both of them, but he wouldn't be that vindictive. What would he do, though, to teach them both a lesson? The decision, as always, was his.

Footsteps sounded in the hall and Erin listened and waited, but they continued on and the door next to hers closed firmly. She bowed her head and a tear welled up and trailed down her pale cheek, but she was even too tired to cry.

After a long time, she started to prepare for bed. Packing could wait until morning. The few things she had brought with her wouldn't take long to put in the suitcase, and the beautiful wardrobe he had provided would, of course, remain in the closet.

Should she leave a note for Bibi? Erin paused. No, it would be better just to disappear. With a heavy heart, she opened a drawer, and there looking up at her was the beautiful lavender peignoir set. It seemed to symbolize the fragility of all her hopes, and she stared at it for a long moment. She had sworn never to wear it, but what difference did it make now? Almost in a dream, Erin slipped the exquisite gown over her head. It settled with a sigh of seduction around her slim body. The delicate lace top permitted alluring glimpses of her firm breasts, and the narrow satin ribbons caressed her shoulders sensuously.

Remembering her impression when she first saw the gown—that it was meant to be seen but not slept in—Erin's mouth twisted with bitter amusement. That had been only the first of a series of mistaken ideas.

Turning off the lights, she walked over to the

window and stared out at the tropic night. It was so beautiful. Tomorrow night at this time she would be back home, and her view would be a small patch of garden instead of this romantic scene. Would she ever again be able to look at the ocean without remembering Jason's handsome face and strange gray eyes so full of conflicting emotions? And would time erase the memory of his hard, lean body pressed so urgently against her own? Erin bowed her head despairingly and the moonlight played with her hair, turning it into shifting shades of fire.

Suddenly there was a click, and a slice of light bisected the darkened room. A man appeared in the doorway, silhouetted by the light at his back. Jason had made his decision! Erin stood completely still, her lips slightly parted. Knowing instinctively that this time there would be no reprieve, her tense body tried to prepare itself.

Her heart beat wildly in her breast as she tried to see his face, but the light was at his back and showed the delicate contours of her wide-eyed face instead. Would she see love in his eyes—or hatred? Would it be a gentle possession or would it be a repeat of that savage night such a short time ago? Her youthful body, so provocatively revealed by the diaphanous gown, started to tremble as she heard his harsh intake of breath.

Suddenly, he sprang at her like a panther and his rough hands started to explore her body. His mouth clamped down on hers in a kiss that was wild and passionate, and Erin almost fainted from the shock. It wasn't Jason. It was *Brad!*

She recoiled in disgust and struggled frantically. "Let go of me, you drunken brute! What are you doing here?"

Instead of answering, he pulled her head back, exposing her white neck. Raining kisses on her

shoulders and throat, his burning lips moved down
to the shadowed area between her breasts.

"I have to have you," he muttered thickly.
"You're driving me wild."

She beat on his chest with tiny, ineffectual fists.
"Take your hands off me, you disgusting beast!"

But her struggles only served to excite him further. "Go on and fight, you little vixen. It won't do
you any good, but I like spirit in my women."

His face was swollen with desire, and Erin knew
fear for the first time. At first she had only been
revolted, not really believing that he would actually
force himself on her once he knew she was unwilling.
But the raw passion in his eyes convinced her and
she was suddenly terrified. Her struggles intensified,
but she was completely helpless against his demonic
strength.

In desperation, she dug her fingernails into his
face. He only laughed and pinned both her hands
behind her back. She tried frantically to twist out of
his grasp, but he held her in a viselike grip. His
heavy, determined hand tugged at her shoulder
strap. As she heard the fragile fabric tear, exposing
one rounded breast, Erin screamed—a high, thin cry
of pure terror.

Then, like an answered prayer, the lights went on
and a strong hand grabbed Brad's collar, yanking
him away. It was Jason, and, like Brad, the mask of
civilization had slipped from his face. With a swift,
brutal jab, his fist lashed out and Brad sprawled on
the floor looking dazed.

Jason stood over him, his face black with fury as
he clenched and unclenched his fists. "Get up, you
louse, because I'm going to kill you!"

Brad was a sorry sight. Erin's scratches were
visible on his cheek, and he rubbed his bruised jaw
tentatively as he struggled to his feet. The blow had

sobered him somewhat, and he had the grace to look shamefaced. "I'm sorry, Jase, I didn't know you and she . . ."

Jason started toward him with such murder in his eyes that Erin was frightened. Putting her hand on his arm she said, "Jason, no! Please . . . just get rid of him."

Brad didn't wait to see how Jason would accomplish this request. Making good use of the unexpected intervention, he scrambled for the door in a most undignified fashion.

It wasn't until the door closed after him that delayed reaction set in and Erin started to tremble uncontrollably.

Jason put his hands on her shoulders, looking at her in deep concern. "Darling, are you all right?" Then the tears came and he took her in his arms. "That's right, my love, let it all out." Stroking her hair gently, he crooned, "You're safe now. I'll never let anything happen to you again."

Even after her sobs subsided, Erin clung to him. He soothed her like a little child, patting her back and murmuring little endearments.

Finally, she raised a tear-stained face and said, "Oh, Jason, I was so scared."

He kissed her cheek, tasting the salty tears. "Why didn't you call me?"

Her eyes were like rain-washed cornflowers as she said simply, "You didn't believe me the first time. I was afraid maybe you'd think I'd . . . encouraged him."

He groaned and folded her tightly in his arms. "I've been a real fool and it's going to take the rest of my life to make amends. How could I ever have doubted you? You're such an innocent child, and I put you in an impossible situation. Can you ever forgive me, my darling?"

There was such tenderness in his eyes that Erin thought she would die of happiness. It was almost worth the agony of this past week to have all the misunderstandings between them cleared up like this.

"It wasn't your fault. Brad is your friend. Naturally you wouldn't believe he'd do anything really dishonorable."

"That wasn't it at all. I'd believe *anything* about Brad," Jason said grimly. "Don't you know why I was so angry with you?" When she shook her head, he explained. "I was blind jealous! I know how Brad operates. Deep down, I always believed you about that scene on the beach, but I did think you were attracted to him. You were always dancing with him—laughing with him. It drove me wild."

She looked at him wonderingly. "I only wanted to be with you, but you seemed to prefer Veronica. You paid more attention to her," she added.

He laughed as he looked at her full pouting lips and the masses of auburn waves tumbling around her lovely face. "Who is Veronica?" he teased, and his mouth covered hers, gently at first and then with increasing urgency.

Sweet surrender swept Erin's body as he strained her close and she felt his lean, muscular hardness through the flimsy material of her gown. Her lips parted under the insistence of his, and he probed her mouth with a male dominance that left her weak. Her arms went around his neck and she was consumed with a longing as old as time.

When he reached up and disengaged her arms, she looked at him blindly, her ragged breathing matching his.

"If I don't stop now, I'll never stop," he told her. "You're very potent medicine, my little love goddess."

Erin's long eyelashes fluttered before the flame in his eyes and she blushed, realizing how readily she had responded. He was the one who had called a halt, not she. He was being honorable, releasing her from her obligation, but she had made a promise and had to be as honorable as he. There was something she had to say and it wasn't easy, but she made herself do it.

"I'm sorry this week didn't work out the way you expected. I know it was my fault. I told you the other night that I . . . couldn't go through with the bargain." Her head drooped, but she forced herself to continue. "I just wanted to say . . . I'm ready now."

There was complete silence. Finally Erin looked up, her cheeks flaming from the effort her surrender had cost. He was gazing at her with such love that her heart missed a beat.

"You poor baby! Did you honestly think I expected you to go through with it?" At her look of complete bewilderment, he took her in his arms, but only for a moment. Putting her resolutely at arms length, he said, "I've been in love with you since you came to my home in Miami and stood up to me in the garden like a small, enraged kitten." He cupped her cheek lovingly in his palm. "I misjudged you then, too, didn't I, my darling? Why do you put up with me?"

It came out spontaneously, and she couldn't have stopped it if she'd tried. "Because I love you," she said without shame.

"Oh, Erin, don't say that, or I'll never get the rest of the story out!" He twisted a silken curl around his fingers. "I never met a girl like you. I was in love with you and I couldn't get to first base. You wouldn't even go out with me. I installed you in my office, where at least I could see you every day, but that was a mixed blessing. You were so thorny.

Sometimes I'd think you were thawing, but then you'd turn cold and distant again."

Remembering her unfounded suspicions about him and Helen, Erin was remorseful. "I misjudged you, too, Jason." There would be time enough later to confess the reason.

"So when this thing about Bob came up, I seized the opportunity. I'm going to take that young man in hand and straighten him out when we get back," he digressed, and Erin could only look at him gratefully.

This week had taught her a lot about strength and weakness. As much as she loved her brother, she was willing to shift the burden.

"I thought if I could force you to spend a week getting to know the real me, maybe I could make you love me just a fraction as much as I love you. I asked Bibi and Tommy to join us as chaperones so there wouldn't be any talk." He ran a hand ruefully through his thick hair. "It was a great plan, but then Brad and Veronica showed up. It was all downhill from there."

Erin was having difficulty assimilating all of this information. "Do you mean you didn't expect me to . . . but you said if I didn't, that Bob . . ." her words trailed off helplessly.

He held her anxious face in his hands and kissed her lightly on the tip of her nose. "How would it look if I sent my own brother-in-law to prison?"

It took a minute for the words to sink in. He was asking her to marry him! She looked at him with starry eyes. "Do you really mean it? Please don't say it if you don't mean it!"

His possessive look was answer enough, but he said, "You couldn't get away from me if you tried!"

Impulsively, she started to fling her arms around his neck, but he stopped her. Reaching for the torn wisp of lace, he kissed her soft skin and his fingers caressed her briefly before he covered her bare breast.

"Don't tempt me too far, little doll. I'm a very normal male and I might elope with you before the big wedding Aunt Harriet is cooking up. She'd never forgive me. She's already making out guest lists and planning the festivities."

Erin was incredulous. "You mean you told her we were going to be married before you even told me?"

"Do you mind?"

Her arms stole around his neck in spite of his halfhearted attempts to resist, and her fervent kiss gave him the answer.

Silhouette Romance

IT'S YOUR OWN SPECIAL TIME

Contemporary romances for today's women.
Each month, six very special love stories will be yours
from SILHOUETTE. Look for them wherever books are sold
or order now from the coupon below.

$1.50 each

$1.75 each

SILHOUETTE BOOKS, Department SB/1

1230 Avenue of the Americas
New York, NY 10020

Please send me the books I have checked above. I am enclosing
$_____ (please add 50¢ to cover postage and handling. NYS and
NYC residents please add appropriate sales tax). Send check or
money order—no cash or C.O.D.'s please. Allow six weeks for delivery.

NAME_____

ADDRESS_____

CITY_____ STATE/ZIP_____

Silhouette Romance

15-Day Free Trial Offer
6 Silhouette Romances

6 Silhouette Romances, free for 15 days! We'll send you 6 new Silhouette Romances to keep for 15 days, absolutely free! If you decide not to keep them, send them back to us. You pay nothing.

Free Home Delivery. But if you enjoy them as much as we think you will, keep them by paying the invoice enclosed with your free trial shipment. We'll pay all shipping and handling charges. You get the convenience of Home Delivery and we pay the postage and handling charge each month.

Don't miss a copy. The Silhouette Book Club is the way to make sure you'll be able to receive every new romance we publish before they're sold out. There is no minimum number of books to buy and you can cancel at any time.

This offer expires May 31, 1982